Alphas of the Underworld:
Embracing the Vampire Prince

MILENA FENMORE

CHAPTER ONE

A flowing, soft, white gown whipped around her hourglass figure, a body many women envied and men salivated for. Her long golden hair flowed behind her as the wind picked up speed. Tara looked from left to right, her oval face with electric blue eyes and scarlet colored lips showing her confusion. She reached a hand up and placed a longish red nail between her teeth, nibbling it, trying to concentrate. Tara always loved the color red. Most of the clothes she wore were different shades of red with dozens of shoes to match. However, never in a million years would she have imagined that the color red had some significance to her destiny.

On her right was Mikael, standing at a strapping almost seven feet, with broad shoulders and a super muscular physique; the epitome of the leader he was. With fiery green eyes that bore into her soul, he waited. His long dark hair also whipped in the wind, while his black silk shirt, opened all the way down, revealed his hard torso. She could see the passion in his face, with his jaw set, feet apart, and ready for war.

She closed her eyes to shut him out, not wanting to think about him. A pain sliced through her at the thought of the situation and what she had to do. She had to make a decision fast or there would be war. Briefly, she wondered what the hell she did to deserve this. Why was she being pulled in all directions? What was the purpose for this?

Then, there was Leon, just about an inch shorter that Mikael. Curly, reddish-brown hair, framed his strong features with eyes that changed color between striking yellow and blazing blue. She had no idea why they did that. He was equally powerfully built, with a face that made you want to touch him. The only trouble was, she had to choose her destiny.

She opened her eyes and looked from one to the other. On the one hand was the man she knew was her soul mate, and on the other was the one who betrayed her. If she chose the one she loved, she could lose him in a war. However, choosing the one she hated in order to stop a war would also bring anguish, not only to her, but to him as well. Tara had to choose between the love of a man and the love of her adopted clan, or go with the one she most detested. She closed her eyes to think…only for a second, then she moved towards her destiny.

*****

Three weeks ago….

Tara placed one foot on the pavement, her long curvy legs clad in three inch scarlet stilettos. Before she could step fully from her red Porsche 911 Carrera, it seemed like a mob accosted her, thronging around the car like bees to flowers in the spring. Startled, she cringed.

"Miss McAllister, please give us a statement!" A male reporter shoved a mike precariously close to door.

"Miss Tara, what can you say about your father's situation?" A female with burgundy highlights on brown hair shoved her way through.

"What will happen to your father's business?" another woman shouted above the cackle of voices.

"Will the investors get back their money?" the first man with thick, black-rimmed glasses asked.

Tara pulled her leg back into her car and slammed the door shut. "Ugh!" she groaned, resting her forehead on the beige, leather-bound steering

5

wheel. She had been so preoccupied that she hadn't seen the throng when she parked.

After a few minutes, she took a chance and peered over the dashboard through the windscreen and noticed the mob was still present. Luckily, her windows were tinted midnight black, limiting their view of the inside of the vehicle. She rested her head back on the wheel, her mind trying to come up with a plan.

She was in front of her apartment building, and she knew there were reporters also waiting for her inside. She had a date in three hours and needed to shower and change. There was no way she could leave her car without some distraction and there was nowhere to go.

Tara McAllister, the social butterfly, now in this situation because the investment firm her father founded was under investigation for fraud after millions of dollars of investors' money went missing. Rumors started circulating that David Hall, a senior broker in the firm, absconded with the company's money. He was supposed to be on vacation, but when the FBI tried to contact him, he was nowhere to be found. His house and car were already sold off and his bank account cleaned out. They suspected that he may have lodged the money in an offshore account.

Her phone began vibrating in her purse. She lifted her head and brushed her long golden tresses from her face, then picked the phone out, swiping her index ginger across the bottom of the touch screen.

"Hello," she whispered.

"Tara?" It was Jared, her boyfriend of three months.

"Jared? I'm so glad you called, please…," she started to say, but Jared was also speaking.

She stopped talking and listened, the blood draining from her face. "I don't think this is going to work out," he was saying, but Tara didn't think she was hearing correctly.

"What are you talking about, Jared?" she tried not to raise her voice but failed.

"Let's not see each other anymore," he replied and there was a click.

"Jared," Tara said into the phone. "Jared?" there was no answer. "You prick!" she flung the device on the front passenger seat and leaned her head back. "Fricking jerk!"

Frustrated and with no idea how to get out of the car without being trampled by the press, she pushed the seat back and relaxed. Might as well make the most of the situation, she thought. She would have driven back out, but her gas tank was low and she had no money. Her memory flashed to that afternoon at Saks Fifth Avenue.

"Sorry Miss Tara, your father's credit line has been cancelled," the brown-haired store clerk said, her brown eyes pitiful. "You can pay with credit your card."

She opened her purse, pulled out the gold card, and handed it over. "Here," she smiled at the woman.

After a minute or two, the clerk looked sadly at her, "I'm sorry Miss Tara.. It's been declined."

Frantically, she pulled out card after card, until she had handed over a total of nine credit cards, which were all useless. She couldn't even get gas at the pump with her gas card. The attendant, who has always been super nice, almost ignored her. His face was serious as he told her that her card was basically useless there. When you're rolling in dough, everyone is your friend, and when you need them the most, you're alone, the thought crossed her mind. She made a mental note to remember each of those people when she was back to her usual wealthy, socialite self.

Tara shuddered at the memory of the most embarrassing day she'd ever had. Not only were her cards denied, she had no cash. The press followed her everywhere. Now, she was stuck, with no gas in her car and no money.

Her father could not help her. It was his money she'd been living on, and now, all his assets have been seized.

Her phone buzzed again and she felt around the seat for it. "Hello?"

"Tara, my dear," he father's rich tone spoke softly to her.

"Daddy, what's happening to us?" a lump rose to her throat and she felt the tears rise as well.

"Don't worry my daughter. Things will be alright," he assured her. "We're just going through a rough patch. Everything will be sorted."

"Daddy, did they find that thief who stole the company's money?"

Her father went silent for a minute, "No dear, they're still looking for him. Tara," he paused. "You may have to get a job, just for a little while."

"A job?" What would she do? She'd never worked a day in her life. She hadn't gone to college because her grades were below par.

"Yes dear, or…," he paused again.

"Or what Daddy?"

"You may have to get married."

"No, daddy! I won't get married. I'll find a job, you'll see," she almost shouted it.

She'd rather work her manicured fingers off rather than get married to someone she didn't love. When she was dating Jared, she had thought that they would fall in love and eventually get married. After three months of dating, there was no chemistry and his kisses were wet and passionless. She liked him well enough, that's why she went out with him, but in the back of her mind, she knew he was only seeing her because of her family's background.

She talked to her father for a while longer while he told her his plans to move to the beach house, which was in her mother's name. The mansion her parents occupied was also seized until this David person was caught. According to the feds, George McAllister, the owner and president of the company, held the ultimate responsibility to his clients to make sure their money was returned to them.

The apartment she lived in was leased in her name through her father's connections. She worried that she might not be able to meet the rent. Her father was right. If she wanted to keep her independence, she must find a job to cover the rent and food. She could not move in with her parents. It was out of the question. Cupertino was where she grew up and wanted to live. Moving to San Benito was not in her plans.

Around midnight, as hungry as a diamond without a carat, Tara looked through the windscreen and saw that the coast was clear. She should have insisted on an apartment building with private parking, but she had been desperate to get out of the house and on her own. This was one of the first apartments she liked and said yes before it got snatched by someone else. She softly opened the door a crack and peered outside. The coast was clear so she pulled off her shoes and ran from her parking space through the entrance of the building.

When she came off the elevator at her floor, she stood for a moment, looking in the direction of the apartment door. It was clear as well. With a sigh of relief, she quickly got to her door, opened it, and stepped inside. One inside her apartment, Tara crumpled on the sofa, confused as to how she would fend for herself. She could move back to her parent's beach house, but that was the last thing she wanted to do. She didn't want to be that daughter than ran back home to her parents because daddy was no longer able to pay the rent. Moreover, her parents had some serious issues to deal with.

She was hungry. The only thing in the apartment to eat was some apples. She liked apples, so there were always those there. In the refrigerator was water and orange juice, nothing more. She picked up an apple from a bowl on the table and went to grab a bottle of spring water from the fridge. There were exactly two left, so she poured half of one bottle in a cup and bit into the apple.

""So, this is what it's like to be poor," she muttered.

With her apple and her water for supper, Tara went to bed, determined to find a way to survive.

* * * *

She stopped and stared. There was a yellow and red lock on her front left car wheel. On the windscreen was a sticky note from the feds, declaring that they were now in possession of her ride. It was the following morning and Tara decided to go job hunting. She'd never done that before, but how hard could it be? There were the want ads in the newspaper. Plus, she was beautiful and popular. Who would refuse to work with her?

"This is not happening!" Tara's heart fell.

She felt like throwing herself on the pavement and lying there until her troubles were over. What now? She needed to find a job somewhere and she had no idea how to get there without a car. There was no money in her purse to call a cab. She was so broke. She couldn't even call a cab. Her last resort was asking her mother for money. She knew some funds were put away for a rainy day, and now, it was raining on Tara. She dialed her mother's number and paced the concrete beside her car.

"Hello?" her mother's voice was the usual, quiet and soft.

"Mom?"

"Tara, honey, where are you?"

"I'm at my apartment mom. They locked my car and placed a sticker on it mom. I have no car, mommy!"

Her mother's tone lifted at the sob in her voice, "Tara, come with us. We're moving in a couple of days."

"No, Mom," she felt like she was choking. "I have got to find a job. I just need some money to keep me for a few days, until I find something."

"Well honey, I'll drop by with some cash later. Wait at home for me."

With hope that her mother was bringing her some money, Tara went back inside to twiddle her thumbs and wait. The day went by slowly, and by noon, she was starving. Another apple and some water was all she'd had for breakfast. There wasn't even coffee in the kitchen and she was badly craving caffeine.

Around four in the afternoon, a knock at the door caused her to spring to her feet. With her stomach churning, she yanked the door open, "Mom what took you so…." Her voice trailed off.

Standing in the doorway was a red faced young man, of no more than twenty two, holding a small package. "Miss Tara," his voice was soft and low. "Your mother asked me to deliver this to you." He handed her the packet and lowered his eyes.

"Thanks," she replied, taking the small brown package.

As the young man walked away, Tara closed the door, then tore open the brown wrapper on the small box. Inside was a note and an envelope with money. She picked up the note and placed the box on the coffee table. 'Use wisely,' was written in her mother's hand writing.

"That's it?" Tara placed the note on the table and counted the money.

She counted two thousand dollars. Tara had never had to budget before and two thousand dollars didn't seem like much. That was less than what she paid for a Gucci handbag. What could two thousand dollars do? She had no clue. The day was already far spent, so she resolved that she would start searching for a job in the morning. However, for now, she needed to eat. She could at least make cereal and she did learn how to make a good salad. So, grocery shopping was the only thing on the agenda for the evening.

CHAPTER TWO

The man looked at her intently. He had one brow up and his lips pursed tightly. Tara smiled and watched as his eyes took her in. She knew that he found her to be attractive, and she would never have dreamed of using her looks to get a job, but this was an emergency. She leaned forward ever so slightly and his eyes lowered.

"So, when can I start?" she asked the man interviewing her.

This was her fourth interview for the position of receptionist. This office was located on the side of town she hated. There was no underground parking there and the noise was almost deafening. She had to take a taxi and the people on the street were always hurrying. The shops sold cheap knockoffs and the place smelled.

"Miss...," he looked down at the form she filled out. "Miss McAllister, you filled out your occupation as socialite and expert shopper, care to explain that?"

Her spirits lifted. None of the other interviewers asked her about her occupation as she had filled it out on the forms. "I know how to socialize. I am popular and I am sure my social skills and social standing in the community will be an asset to your company," she smiled brightly. "And I know how to spot a fake from a mile off. Like that suit, you probably were ripped off. It looks like a Zegna brand, but it's not."

The man blushed, "Well, Miss McAllister, I appreciate your kind of talent, but this is a Stationery Distribution company. I think your talents are better suited elsewhere."

"Does that mean I don't get the job?"

He smiled and nodded, "I'm sorry. Good luck with your next interview."

Tara's face fell. She looked at the man behind the desk and noticed that he seemed to be trying hard not to laugh. Was he making fun of her? She stood with a pout and straightened her skirt which clung to her curves like a second skin. Her small waist tapered out, making a perfect curve outward and then slanted inward toward her thighs, the perfect shape of a seductive woman.

She was wearing a pink skirt suit with a navy blouse. Her short jacket opened up at the front and the blouse had a dipping neckline that showed a little more cleavage than it should. The man's eyes followed her as she straightened her collar and brushed an imaginary flint from the front of her jacket. His eyes lingered on her full package and his mouth opened slightly. Tara could almost see the saliva trickling from his lips.

"Thank you for your time, sir," Tara walked away rather slowly, knowing he was watching her butt. She could almost hear him gulp and see him loosen his tie, knowing how uncomfortable he was at that moment. He was probably nursing a hard-on under his desk.

She knew her body made men weak. She had been told that many times. They didn't hide how they felt and she knew what to do to make men's eyes pop out of their heads. Tara was one of those girls that knew how to act all sexy and experienced, yet she'd never fully given herself to anyone. Second base was as far as she'd gone with any man she'd dated. Her philosophy was 'look, but touching should be reserved for love'.

"This is much harder than I thought," she said to herself while walking through the front office of the distribution center.

The next on her list was a club downtown called 'The X Zone'. She had no idea what she would be doing there but she called a cab and took the ride. It was around eleven when she arrived so the place seemed empty. The inside had an eerie feel to it. The lights were dim and a weird droning music played over speakers on the wall.

"Can I help you?" a girl with a grim expression and a flat voice asked.

"I came about a job. I saw an ad in the wanted section," she replied, a chill running up her spine and the dead look in the girl's eyes.

"Oh, wait here," the girl's equally dead sounding voice replied, walking off towards what appeared to be a passage towards the back of the dark room.

At the bar to the left, a blond hair man was doing something, she wasn't sure what. He raised his head once to look at her and went back to his task. Then, she noticed the tables were enclosed in booths for privacy and in the center was the dance floor. To the far back, near to where the girl had disappeared to, was what appeared to be a stage with a pole.

Soon after, a tall fellow appeared. He was wearing a red jacket and his dark hair was slicked back. His beady black eyes raked over her as he approached. Her skin crawled at his perusal but she stood her ground and waited for him to speak.

"Where have you worked before?" he was walking around her, looking at her from head to toe.

"I…well…," she hesitated, not sure what to say.

"Okay, show me what you got. Ryan," he turned to the bartender. "Put some music on."

"Wait," Tara was confused. "What am I supposed to do?"

"Dance, little lady, dance," he grinned. "Would you prefer to use the stage?" he motioned towards the back where the stage was.

"I don't dance. I thought you needed a waitress," she turned to leave.

That's when she saw him. He was leaning against the door frame at the entrance to the club. The morning sunlight bouncing off his red hair looked like flames on his head. With his back to the light, she could not see his face, but she felt his presence. She could not move, yet she could not peel her eyes away from his wide shoulders. He seemed to swallow up the doorway with his stature. He was the tallest man she'd ever seen.

He moved, raising himself from his relaxing position by the door and glided her way. She stood transfixed as her eyes drank in his magnificence. He was coming straight towards her and she braced herself. Shoulders straight, chin up, and a smile that could light a Christmas tree.

"Ryan," his easy drawl called out to the bartender. "One special, make it spicy." He passed her and her heart sank. Tara took a shaky breath and started towards the door. "Give the lady whatever she wants, that is, if she'll join me."

She stopped, not sure if he was talking about her, but there was no one else in the bar, except for the girl from earlier. She turned and he was seated at one of the tables. He motioned to the seat beside him with a sly smile. Tara looked at the cocky bastard and how he leaned back in the chair, his smile plastered confidently on his face, and his eyes, how they twinkled. She'd never seen that before. There seemed to be something in his eyes that glinted, like embers.

She shook her head from the mesmerizing effect and turned towards the door. Her gut told her that she needed to get out of there fast.

"Are you scared?" he asked, as if mocking her.

She twirled and looked directly into his eyes. "No. I don't drink with strangers," then she walked away.

By the time she was shielding her eyes from the bright California sun, a shadow loomed over her. Tara looked up and met hypnotic sapphire eyes. There were flecks of yellow in there somewhere which disappeared quickly. With great effort, she pulled her gaze away, stepped around him, and hailed

15

a taxi, getting in as quickly as possible.

As she rode the taxi downtown, Tara flashed back to a few minutes earlier and the handsome face of the stranger. His prominent bone structure and strong nose were memorable to say the least. In all her going out on the town, her life as a socialite, she'd never met someone so alluring. He also moved with lighting speed, since he was able to get outside before her, enough to block her path, yet she never saw him pass by her. There must have been another exit, she thought.

Her next stop was another club Downtown, called 'The Underground'. It was located in the basement of one of the buildings in the business district. The entrance was located at the back of the building with a large burly fellow dressed in a black t-shirt and black pants, guarding the door. When she walked up to him, he reached out a hand to block her path.

"I'm here to see Charlie about the waitress job," she smiled sweetly at him and batted her eyes. The fellow dropped his hand and nodded towards the door. "Thanks," she said.

It was a twenty-four hour club, and they seemed to need waitresses to serve on shifts. When she entered, a young girl a few inches shorter than she was escorted her to a back office. The place was fairly well lit with yellow fluorescent bulbs. There was a long bar to one side with a dark-haired man behind the counter.

"Welcome," a raspy female voice said as soon as the stepped inside the spacious room with a glass top desk and a high back leather chair. There was a bookshelf on one wall and a sofa bed against the opposing wall. She looked around to see where the voice was coming from, and as if out of nowhere, a tall dark-haired woman with porcelain skin, red flaming hair, and indigo eyes appeared before her.

"Hi, I'm Tara," she smiled awkwardly, feeling intimidated by the penetrating gaze of the woman.

"I'm Charlie, come in," the woman, not much older than she, indicated a chair near her desk. "I'm the manager. My brother Leon owns the place."

She handed Tara a form to fill out, nothing major, just basic information. There was no real interview. She asked a few basic questions about her experience and that was it. Tara was as honest as possible and felt comfortable with Charlie.

"Your office is nice," Tara remarked. It was a comfortable space, unlike any office she'd seen in a club. The room could easily be mistaken for an executive's office.

"Ah, yes, Leon likes extravagance," she smiled and her sparkly white teeth showed a spot of red, where her scarlet lipstick might have smeared. "Have you worked as a waitress before?" she asked.

Tara briefly thought of lying, but those eyes bored into her that she felt compelled to tell the truth. "No," she replied in a quiet voice, folding her hands in her lap.

"Don't worry, it's easy, just balance the tray and don't break anything," Charlie laughed. "When can you start?"

Tara's face lit up, "Right away!"

"Alright, so long as Leon is okay with it. You can hang out in the club tonight to get a feel of how things are done. Start taking orders when you feel comfortable. I've got to go out for a while so make yourself at home."

Charlie disappeared much the same way that she appeared. One minute she was there, and as soon as Tara lowered her eyes, she was gone. It was disconcerting, but she was elated that she found a job. She went back to the club room and hung out while the other waitresses filed in. They were wearing short black skirts and black tank tops. They all seemed to be pale looking, like they've never been out in the California sun. It was strange because even Tara, who didn't expose herself much, had a slight tan.

She was busy watching the waitresses set up the tables when someone walked up behind her, "I see we meet again, maybe now you'll have that drink?"

Tara turned. Her eyes met with the man she'd seen at the other club. "Are you stalking me?" she hissed.

"Maybe, how about that drink?"

"I told you. I don't drink with strangers," she made to walk away when one of the waitresses walked up.

"Leon, Charlie said she'll be back later, that you should take care of the new hire," the young woman with the name tag 'Grace' on it, glanced her way, then walked went back to work.

"You're Leon?" she asked, confused.

"Yes, now we are no longer strangers," he grinned and stretched his hand out for her to take.

Tara looked at the hand and hesitantly placed hers in his large one. Leon brought it to his lips and let it linger there a moment. She pulled her hand away, turning red with embarrassment. She could feel the eyes of the waitresses on her and she shuffled uncomfortably.

"I'm Tara. I'm the new waitress. I need to get to work," her voice was a bit shaky.

"No need to rush," Leon remarked, snapping his fingers to get the attention of one of the girls. "Bring me a special and something for Tara here," he turned to her. "What will it be?"

"Do you think it's a good idea fraternizing with the new hireling?" she asked in a low tone. She didn't think it was such a good idea.

"Is there a reason why I can't drink with my employees?" he asked with one eyebrow raised. "If it bothers you that much, we can make it into an interview of sorts. What do you think?" He asked, offering her a seat.

"Okay," she replied with a wary smile. "I'll have mineral water."

"That's it?" Leon looked taken aback. "You look like a girl with higher standards. I'm surprised."

"I can't drink while I'm on the job, trust me," she told him. "Let's just say, my alcohol tolerance is near zero."

The waitress, Grace, brought a tall glass with what appeared to be a Bloody Mary, garnished with a stalk of celery, and her mineral water. She immediately took a sip to sooth her suddenly dry throat.

Leon laughed. A booming sound that reverberated through the room. The two waitresses looked on with interest and smiled. He leaned forward, his eyes travelling over her face, lingering on her lips. After a few seconds, they dropped to her bosom and stuck there.

"No worries, you will be safe here," she heard him say, his eyes never leaving her breasts.

She grew red again. Leon was brazen to say the least, she thought. He made no effort to hide the fact that he was undressing her. She shifted uncomfortably in her seat.

"So, tell me, why a girl like you wants to be a waitress?"

Finally, his eyes lifted and looked directly into hers. She wanted to hide the truth, but something about his gaze told her that the truth was better. That he would know she was lying.

"My family's assets were seized by the feds. I need to get a job to survive until it's over," she uttered, taking another sip of water and trying to avoid his eyes.

"I like how honest you are. I really like you, from the moment I saw you," he leaned forward. "Let me take care of you."

"What?"

"Let's not waste time. Go out with me. Pretend you met me under other circumstances and I asked you out on a date, would you say yes?"

She hesitated to answer. When she'd seen him earlier, he looked magnificent, like the way he looked now. She had to admit that he was quite handsome, perhaps the most handsome man she'd ever seen. His presence seemed to fill the room, but she couldn't shake the feeling that he spelled danger.

"Yes, I would,' she found herself replying.

"Then let's forget about you being a waitress and let's date," he declared. "We'll take it slow."

Her heart started to beat heavily and her face went red once more. Tara wasn't sure whether or not she should take a chance on a guy she just met. Yet again, that's how people dated wasn't it? You meet someone, there's a connection, and you go out.

"Okay," she didn't even realize when she consented.

"Now, have a proper drink," he insisted.

She ordered a dirty martini with two olives. Leon told her a story of a fight that happened the night before, how the two men had mistakenly started to fight over a girl that none of them knew. It was funny because one guy was drunk enough to think the woman was his girlfriend who broke up with him a month before. The other guy was just minding his own business when the first guy attacked him and accused him of hitting on his woman. She knew he was trying to put her at ease and she started to relax.

They talked about her father's company and he told her that everything was going be alright. With everything that happened to her family, he was the first person to tell her that, and it made her feel better. The conversation moved from her to the city, to the business, and back to her.

"I see you've stolen my waitress," it was Charlie returning from wherever she'd been.

Tara looked around and saw that the place was bustling with activity. It was strange that, while talking with Leon, she hadn't realized that there was activity around her. He'd totally pulled her in and shut out the outside world.

"She's worth stealing," he remarked and grinned at his sister.

A look passed between the two that she did not understand. Tara wondered how many girls that came to work there he'd actually 'stolen'. Was it a habit of his to date the waitresses or was she special? Her questions must have been evident on her face because Leon reached over and engulfed her hand in his.

"Don't worry. I don't do this often. It's different with you," he drawled.

CHAPTER THREE

Tara insisted on working as a waitress to earn wages though Leon wanted to date exclusively and take care of her. For her, that was moving a little too fast for her taste. She liked him a lot, but the chemistry was taking a while to build. She figured that perhaps she was apprehensive about letting herself feel because of what Jared did. Then again, she didn't quite trust Leon, not yet anyway.

He was gorgeous, with his sapphire eye that had flecks of yellow in there. Those were the most unusual eyes she'd ever seen. He was also the tallest man she'd met to date, almost seven feet, she estimated, with broad powerful shoulders and wonderfully toned forearms. She hadn't yet seen his body, but she could imagine what he looked like without a shirt, though she refused to think about his lower extremities.

He had wanted to tell everyone she was his girlfriend, but she insisted they keep things light, for now. Waiting tables wasn't so bad and no one bothered her. She earned tips that allowed her to pay her bills while waiting on her weekly check. The pay was good, but she decided to save that and use her tips to live on. What she found extremely jarring about the club was the same drone-like music that played over and over. It sometimes moved at a faster pace but it seemed like the same CD was forever replaying.

The dancing was the same with the patrons. A deathlike dance that made it seem like the people were in a trance. Though curious about it, she never asked why. She figured that perhaps that's what made the club popular, because it was always busy. Perhaps, this particular club was for weird people who liked zombie movies and music.

It was Tuesday, almost a week after starting her new job. Things were looking up. At night, the place was very busy; however, there was something different about this place. She hated the weird background music that played slowly; unlike the usual rock sounds that made you want shake your booty. This grated on her nerves and made her feel like tearing her hair out. Her shift was over and Leon promised to take her home, with Charlie's approval.

"You take care of her. She's valuable," Charlie warned as they headed out the door.

Tara wasn't sure if it was a joke or not, but she smiled and let him place his hand on the small of her back and guided her to his midnight black Ferrari.

"Your carriage awaits my dear," he bowed and let her into the front passenger seat.

He slipped in beside her, reached across her, and buckled her seat belt. She felt heat rise up her neck when his hand brushed her breast. His face was close to her and his lips closer. She knew what he was doing and it was working. They'd gone out for five days but were yet to share a kiss. Though she'd wanted to, she had avoided it at all cost. Now, he was so close, his lips were slightly parted, and she could feel his breath on her face.

"Tara," he whispered, inching closer and there was nothing she could do.

Though she felt cornered, she was looking forward to feeling his lips on hers. She opened her mouth to meet his tongue, which was smooth. It was a sweet kiss that made her flush. A slow warmth spread across her chest and neck, and upwards to her cheeks. She twined her arms around his neck to make the kiss more intimate.

Briefly, Leon pulled away to nibble her neck. "You're so beautiful," he growled.

"You're beautiful too," she mumbled, feeling foolish after saying it.

He came back to her lips and nibbled the corners. Leon pushed the car seat backwards and pressed his chest into her breast.

"What're you doing?' she asked, her breath quite shallow.

"Ravishing you, what else?" he nipped her lips and she felt a little sting there.

She reached her tongue out to soothe the sting and tasted blood. Before she could protest, Leon was sucking on the area and it felt good to her so she relaxed. He then kissed her cheeks and ears. A small ripple of excitement coursed through her but she wasn't ready to go all the way.

"I'm not ready Leon. I need more time," she murmured.

"Neither am I, but I just want to taste you, just a little," he whispered, nibbling her bottom lip.

She had to admit that it felt good. He was an amazing kisser and she wanted him to continue nibbling her lips and stroking her tongue. She'd never been kissed quite like that before and she wanted to savor the moment. His lips and tongue trailed a wet path along her temple and down to the crook of her neck. There, he began to suck on her skin after sniffing and telling her how great she smelled. At first, the sucking was tingly, but as he continued, it became a little painful.

"Leon, what if somebody sees us?" she looked out the window and there were people leaving the club, while others were going in.

"You're right. Let's go somewhere else. We can park the car and kiss all we want," he grinned and started the car, gunning the engine as soon as he pulled away.

He drove to Portal Park which was empty at that time of the night. It was already around eleven thirty. Leon encouraged her to take a leisurely walk and she complied. The night was cool, compared to the earlier temperatures of the day. Tara took her shoes off and walked in the cool grass. It was a first for her, but she felt relaxed doing it. As they went deeper into the park, Leon took her hand, a romantic gesture she appreciated.

Suddenly, he stopped and pulled her into his arms. "I love the taste of your lips," he rumbled.

His lightly kissed the place on her lip that he had bitten before, a light feathery kiss that tingled. He followed through with light feathery kisses on her face and ears, and she sagged into him. He certainly knew how to woo a girl, she thought. He began kissing her neck in earnest, then sucking on the spot he'd been sucking before. It seemed like the exact spot because it felt a little sore.

"It's going to leave a mark, Leon," she protested.

"Yes, and that mark claims you as mine," he raised his head and looked into her eyes. "Be mine, sweet Tara."

"I'm not ready," she declared once more, feeling his hardness pressing into her.

His eyes were changing color, alternating between sapphire and yellow. What she saw there made her begin to fear him. Inside those eyes were yellow sparks, like fire. She'd never seen eyes like that before on any human.

"Oh God," she breathed.

"What's the matter?" Leon inquired.

"Your eyes, they're…," she was confused. "Weird."

"No, these are my normal eyes."

The flames began to burn brighter in them until all of his iris, pupils, and lens were yellow flames, boring into her soul.

"What are you?" she whispered shakily, trying to step out of his grasp, but he held her tightly.

"Oh, I'm the prince of my clan and I am looking for my queen," he stated matter-of-factly.

"Prince? Clan? What do you mean?"

He needn't answer her because she could see the gleam of a pair of fangs as he grinned. Her heart started beating wildly in her chest and her stomach churned in fear. No! Her mind screamed. She should have guessed when all he drank were those red drinks. Nothing more. No food, no nothing, just those red drinks she thought were Bloody Marys. Perhaps, they were the blood of some girl named Mary, but she would be damned if she was going to be his next drink!

"No, get away from me!"

"Be my queen Tara, and you will want for nothing," he said, while trailing a long nail along her jawline.

His fangs were fully out and she could see his real features in the dimness of the light which reflected from one of the lamps in the park. They were at the far end of the park, quite secluded. She wanted to run away but his grasp was strong and her legs would never carry her, because they felt like jelly.

"No, leave me alone!" She shoved him but he was like the rock of Gibraltar, unmoving. "Get away from me!" she tried to scream but her voice came out in a hoarse whisper. "Help me!"

Something in Leon's eyes changed and they became bright orange. If fear could make her fly away, she certainly would have, because she'd never been so scared in her life. Her limbs became weak and she felt nauseated. Even her head was pounding like crazy. A stoned look came over Leon, and with a slow, methodical movement, he dipped his head once more. She felt his lips touch her neck where it met her shoulder, right in the crook. Then, what felt like needles pierced her skin.

"Ouch!" she screamed, but the needles penetrated deeper and she felt weird, like she was floating.

Her pounding head became like feather inside, light and soft. She could feel and hear him sucking her like before, but this was different. She smelled the blood and felt her veins giving away her life juices. She could feel the blood flowing towards her neck where Leon sucked and knew what was happening. Slowly, her head became lighter and her mind lost focus.

She tried to push against him but her attempts were weak. What was happening to her? Why was he doing this? She didn't even get to say goodbye to her parents. She raised a weak hand and raked her nails along his cheek. She felt his skin on her fingertips but he never let her up. He held her as if in a seductive embrace

She began to feel cold as her warm blood left her. But scarier than that, her heartbeat slowed as Leon drained her blood. She didn't feel like she was dying, more so like she was tired. When she could no longer keep her eyes open, she relaxed and let him do as she pleased. Tara closed her eyes, knowing there was nothing she could do about what happened. Then, Leon was kissing her and he tasted funny. Slowly, she sank into oblivion as he continued to ravish her mouth.

CHAPTER FOUR

"Miss," the voice sounded far away. "Miss!" a hand gripped her shoulder and shook her.

"Benny, you think she's dead?" Another voice came through the fog in her brain. "Look, there's a mark on her neck. It looks infected."

"You're right. We gotta call the cops," the one named Benny replied.

Tara groaned. Her joints ached and she felt strange, like she'd been beaten all over. Her eyelids were heavy and it took most of what strength she had to open them. The men jumped back, startled. Their mouths fell open and they looked on as she arose. Her joints creaked as she stretched from what could have been sleep or unconsciousness. The heady, feathery sensation in her head was making her head bob like a puppet, so she twisted her neck back and forth to try and make it steady. For a few seconds, she had no idea where she was, but what she knew was that she felt cold, like she'd been on ice.

They were looking at her with eyes wide open, as if she was some strange sight from another planet. Their rakes and brooms clutched tightly in their hands with the rubbish bin lying on its side behind them. They were the park cleanup crew.

"Y-y-young lady," one of the men stuttered. It sounded like Benny's voice. "Are you okay?"

"Yes," her voice sounded like there was a frog in there somewhere and she cleared her throat. "Yes, I'm okay." She picked up her bag and shoes, stumbled away and walked to the entrance of the park.

It was the break of dawn, the rising sun casting a dull glow over the city. The city lights flickered, soon to be diminished with the dawn of the new day. In a daze, Tara made her way down the empty street, moving like a drunk, staggering and stumbling along the way. She never thought of calling a cab, which she could have. Something vibrated on her and she stopped to check her jeans pocket which had her cell phone and apartment keys. It was the phone alarm going off but why was she in the park at that time of morning? She stopped for a minute to clear her mind, trying to remember what happened.

The memory entered her mind slowly, oozing in like thick gel seeping through a small hole. Leon! The name popped in suddenly, then the glob spread across her brain and a sharp pain shot through her head. She gripped both sides of her head and pressed the heels of her palms into her temples, waiting for the pain to subside. It took several minutes, and then she moved on again.

She barely managed to reach her apartment before the sun was fully up. Once inside, she took a well needed shower and snuggled under the covers, falling asleep almost instantly. When Tara awoke, it was dark out. She wasn't sure how long she'd slept for, but the pain in her head was excruciating. When she tried to get up, a pain in her chest immobilized her. It was like a large machete was stuck in the middle of her chest. The more she moved the more the pain spread through her body.

The agony she was feeling was unlike anything she'd ever felt. Her lungs also seemed to have stopped working because she felt like she couldn't breathe, that she was suffocating. In addition to the throbbing pain pulsing through her, every few minutes, a sharp wave of heat followed by cold washed over her. Her skin felt dry to the touch, yet she felt like she was burning up one minute and freezing the next.

Another attack of pain rocked her body and she let out a loud blood curdling scream that reverberate through the apartment. It happened several times. Tara thought for sure that she was about to die. She curled up on the bed in a fetal position and waited for her fate. Eventually, the pain was so much that she lost consciousness again.

When next she awoke, it was morning. She arose, without pain, and went to the bathroom. There was something off with her. She could feel nothing, neither hot nor cold. She couldn't feel what temperature the water was that ran from the tap. She brushed her teeth and splashed water on her face, then pulled a towel to pat dry.

Slowly, she raised her head and looked in the mirror, but had to do a double take. Tara staggered back at the reflection looking at her. The eyes of the person looking at her were blazing orange, with red blood vessels around the lenses. Her skin was ashen and deathly looking.

"What happened to me?" she closed her eyes and the memory of Leon's kiss penetrated her mind.

Then, she recalled how he'd taken her to the park. They kissed and he told her she was beautiful. He wanted to be with her but she refused. The memory of his fangs as they glowed in the dark stuck with her. She raised a hand and touched her neck where he'd bitten her. There were two holes there. She could see the grey flesh inside her neck and knew that she wasn't the same.

A hollow feeling in the pit of her stomach made her aware that she hadn't eaten since…she had no idea when. She had no idea how long she'd been in this state. She assumed that when she awoke in the park was the morning after being with Leon. That would have made it Wednesday morning. But she had slept until it was dark and now awakened once more. She estimated that this was Thursday but wasn't sure.

She turned the television on and watched for any indication of how much time she had lost. She was right. It was Thursday; two days after Leon assaulted her. Tara was confused. Was this something you reported to the police? Would they laugh at her if she told them that the man she was dating was a vampire and he wounded her with his fangs?

She spent the rest of the day inside her apartment, trying to feed on apples, but her hunger was getting worse. Nothing she ate seemed to fill the void, and by nightfall, she was famished. She went out at around eight to get some food at the nearby deli, but something strange happened. While she was in the deli parking lot, there were three boys. Their voices carried to the opposite end of the lot where she was.

With caution, she stopped to see what was happening and noticed that there seemed to be some sort of jostling between two of them. They appeared to be teen boys of no older than seventeen. Out of curiosity, she inched closer. The one in the orange t-shirt seemed angry and he shouted at the one in the white jersey shirt and matching baseball cap.

"You fracking idiot, you broke it!" The one in the orange shirt screamed, violently shoving the other boy.

His baseball cap fell off and landed on the hard concrete. The third boy had a small device in his hand, fumbling with it and mumbling. Slowly, the one in the cap stood and brushed himself off, then he walked up to the other boy and punched him on the mouth.

"Fuck, you hit me!" he screamed.

"You shoved me!"

The boy raised his hand and touched his lips, "You busted my lips...you jerk!"

There was a trickle of blood running from his bottom lip to his chin. Then, the weirdest thing happened. Tara found herself moving towards the boys, and when she was close the one who threw the punch, he ran off, leaving the other two. She moved closer and he stared at her as she neared him. The boy with the small device hurried away as well.

"Joey, wait for me," he called after the fleeing boy.

"Who are you?" Orange t-shirt asked, fingering his lips and looking into her eyes.

"I'm the one who can make that better," she told the boy. "Do you want me to kiss it and make it better?"

The boy grinned and looked at her breasts. She had pulled on a tight tank and shorts. Her breasts were stretching the fabric to its limits. She flipped her hair back and moved closer and he backed away. Soon she had backed him into a shaded part of the lot where there were no cars parked.

"Let me see," she cajoled in her sweet honey voice.

The boy stood wide eyed as she gripped his chin and pulled his face towards hers. She then stuck her tongue out and licked his bottom lip which had started to swell. Tara wasn't sure what she was doing but she could not stop. Something inside her was propelling her and she gave in. The blood tasted sweet to her and she wanted more. She licked him again and the boy sucked in his breath. She could feel his excitement and this made her feel powerful. Tara dipped her head and sniffed his neck. The sweet smell of his blood penetrated her nostrils, making them flare.

"Carl!" a voice called from across the lot. "CARL!" It was the other boy from earlier, Joey, calling.

Carl broke free and ran towards his friends. Tara felt strange. It was weird what she had done. The taste of the blood lingered on her tongue and in her mind. All she could think of was having more of it. She hurried into the deli and picked up some fruits and a sandwich, then went back to the apartment.

Eating the fruits and sandwich did nothing to appease her hunger. All she could think of was the taste of the blood. Brushing her teeth several times did nothing to get the taste out of her mouth. By bedtime, she knew she would have to fight hard to keep from giving in to her taste buds. It wasn't her tongue that was the problem. It was her mind. She went to bed in an effort to try and sleep it off, thinking that, by morning, she may feel better.

It was no use. Tara awoke in the dark hours of 3 AM with a need so bad she felt like she was going crazy. By this time, her hunger for blood had become a madness and all she wanted was to get a taste…one drop. With a crazed mind, she left her apartment and started running towards the same park that Leon had abandoned her in. There, she roamed for a while trying to prevent herself from doing the unthinkable.

She ended up at the club Underground, where she'd worked for the few days with Leon. With the intention of not being seen, she lurked in a dark corner behind the building until she saw Leon come outside. He had his arms around a girl and was headed to his car.

She ran from her hiding place calling his name, "Leon!"

He turned and looked at her with distaste.

"Who is she?" the girl asked.

"I don't know," he replied.

"You made me like this you sonofabitch!" she shrieked.

"Is she on drugs?" the girl asked.

"Let's go," he shoved the girl in the front passenger seat, ignoring her, and speeding away.

Tara wandered around some more thinking about Leon. Didn't he recognize her? She could feel the changes in her body and wanted him to help her, to tell her what to do. What if she could not contain the urge to feed on human blood? The unthinkable to her was feeding on the blood of a fellow human. "Arghhhhhhhhhhhhhhhh!" she let out a long angry sound.

Her craving was getting worse, like an obsession, and she wasn't sure how much longer she could hold out without seeking some human blood.

She thought of going to back see Leon, but what good would that do? He did this to her and left her for dead. As is, there was nothing she could do about him until she figured out how to deal with being the way she was. Tara roamed around until the wee hours of the morning, then headed back home. She stayed in her apartment, locking the doors, and willing herself not to go out. Most of the day was spent sleeping anyway, so her craving seemed to be under control.

By nightfall, when she arose from sleep, she was hungry, and again, the need for human blood was so strong that she could smell the blood of the neighbors in her apartment. Her senses seemed to have heightened as well, because she could tell when someone was near or when they left the building. This was disconcerting and tiring. Not only could she sense them, but she could also sense their emotions, their fears.

Her head was a jumbled mess. Tara felt like she was going crazy. She looked crazy. Then, it occurred to her that perhaps ending this would be better than living as an undead. Would she never see her parents again? What if seeing them would cause them hurt? Would she crave their blood the way she was craving human blood now? It was too much to take.

Getting through another night was going to be difficult but she was determined to stay inside the apartment. "Just get through this night Tara," she encouraged. "You can do this."

Her phone rang at around eight. "Hello?" she was a bit apprehensive about answering it.

"Tara, honey," her mother's voice soothed her rattled nerves.

"Mom, oh mom!" her voice cracked.

Tara wanted to tell her mother her woes, but her mother would never believe her, or she would insist on her coming home right away.

"Are you alright? Do you need money?" Mrs. McAllister asked, the concern registering in her voice.

"No, Mom, I'm fine," she lied. "I miss you so much."

"How's that job of yours? It's a club isn't it?"

"Yes, it's a club…," she hesitated. "It's fine Mom. Everything is just fine."

How could she tell her mother that her boss, whom she was dating, was a vampire and that he bit her, sucked her blood, and left her for dead?

"Didn't you say the guy who owns the place asked you out? How's that going?" Her mother pressed.

"It did…," she thought better of her answer. "I decided it's not a good idea to date my boss, Mom."

"Oh, that's good. Is he okay with you working with him, seeing you rejected him?" Mrs. McAllister was really pushing for answers about her love life, but Tara had to stay strong.

"Yes, Mom, he's fine with it. I've got to go Mom. I love you," her voice was hoarse.

"Are you sure you're okay? You don't sound so good," a mother's intuition was right on point.

Tara gripped the phone tightly, determined not to let her mother know what was happening. She took a deep breath and cleared her throat. "Yes, Mom," her voice was much clearer now. "I miss you and Daddy, but I'm fine."

Her mother went on to tell her about the progress they were having with finding the man who defrauded the company. The feds were on to something and may have located the bank account. It seemed that very soon, they would have the problem resolved and things may go back to normal. It was good news for her parents. There was some sadness in her voice when she hung up the phone.

She managed to get through the night without going off the deep end, and by morning, she was determined to end the agony. She'd heard stories

35

that vampires cannot go out into the sun, yet she'd seen Leon in the hot California sun the day she met him. Was there some trick to it? She decided to see what would happen. Worst case scenario would be that she catches on fire, which would not be so bad after all. That morning was do or die. She needed an end to her torment and perishing was the only feasible option. Tara had no intention of existing as a vampire.

With her mind made up, she ventured out when the sun was at its zenith. At first, her eyes hurt terribly and it took a while to get adjusted to the glare, but there was no burning sensation, no flames…nothing. She walked around in a daze trying to figure another way to end this.

"Garlic!" she shouted. "That must be true. Vampires are afraid of garlic."

It wasn't true. Tara was able to pick up a whole kilo of the stuff in the supermarket. She held them on her hand and sniffed, but nothing happened. After taking home the bag of garlic, she peeled them all, which was a lot. Placing the cloves in a large bowl, she stayed in front of the television and turned on the movie channel.

"Now, let's see what happens," she murmured, popping a clove into her mouth like popcorn. Soon, the bowl was empty. "Burp," she belched. The air around her stank of the pungent smell of garlic.

Disappointed, she turned the movie off and went to bed hoping to get some well needed sleep. As she hugged her pillow, she felt nauseated. The feeling of wanting to vomit was strong so she sprang from the bed and went to the bathroom, hanging her face over the toilet. The feeling rose to her throat and she hurled, but nothing came up but air. Over and over she hurled, thinking that her innards would come through her mouth at any minute; however, nothing of the sort happened. Eventually, her stomach began to settle and she went back to bed.

"Another lie humans tell about vampires," she muttered.

Tara was confused as what to do. She didn't want this. She never asked for this. Damn Leon! How could he do this to her and leave her? With firm resolve, she left her apartment that night and headed out into the city, trying hard to avoid human contact. When she neared the Cypress Hotel, she stopped. She'd been there many times at functions or on dinner dates. The place held many wonderful memories for her.

She ran to the back and found the workers' exit open. There was a stairwell that led to the roof and she took it, undetected. Once on the roof, she was able to look out over the city. There were lights of various colors sprinkled over the city. They were a beauty to behold, but she had no place there anymore. This was the end for Tara as she moved her feet, one behind the other to the edge of the building.

She wasn't afraid. Rather, she was satisfied that this was the right thing to do. With her eyes closed, she stretched her arms out on either side of her, like wings. Taking a deep breath, she let herself go.

CHAPTER FIVE

Feeling herself float in the air was freeing. The sensation of flying gave her the freedom of knowing she did the right thing. Then, she hit something or was it someone? She couldn't tell with her eyes closed. There was no pain, no splatter, no hitting the pavement like she had anticipated and, NO, she knew she wasn't dead.

"NO, NO, NO, NO NOOOOOOOOOOO!" Tara screamed into the night air, her eyes still tightly shut.

"Let it out. That's good," a deep rich voice shocked her into opening her eyes.

She stared, then blinked and stared into the face of a man with a chiseled jawline. His fiery green eyes were alit, and those flecks of orange, much like Leon's, told her that he too was not human. His long, dark hair hung loosely about his shoulders. She was lying crosswise in his muscular arms. His red silk shirt was open up to his midriff, and her eyes came into contact with hard pecks. Her eyes flicked back to his, which softened, losing the flames as they bored into her.

"Hi," he grinned, showing white pearly teeth.

For a second, she doubted whether he was vampire or not. "Hi," she wiggled from his grasp and got to her feet. "How did you catch me and not get hurt?"

"I've been waiting for you," he stated.

He was even taller than Leon, exuding more power. She was certain he was not human. "Waiting for me?" she asked, confusion showing on her face.

"Yes, you've been confused and hurt. I am here to make things better. Come," he reached his hand out to her.

"No, I'm not falling for that. Did Leon send you?"

"No, Leon is not of my clan. I am Mikael, Leader of Moonlight Hearts Clan."

She hesitated. Leon never told her which clan he belonged to, but this wasn't so bad. If she joined this clan, then she wouldn't have to see him ever again. But, no, she had no desire to be a vampire.

"I'll groom you how to survive in the vampire world," Mikael offered.

"I don't want to be a vampire, to do to people what Leon did to me!" she stepped back.

"You don't have to. You can survive without feeding on humans," he said. "Come, let me teach you."

She didn't quite trust him, "How do I know you are telling me the truth?"

"You can always return to your life if you don't like what I have to offer," he hadn't withdrawn his hand. "You won't die from eating garlic, walking in the sun, and jumping off buildings."

"How'd you know...?"

"Let's just say, we know things that humans don't."

Curiously, she asked, "How do vampires die?"

He smiled, still keeping his hand outstretched for her to take. "Only a vampire can kill a vampire, humans with special gifts, or angels. You have a choice, to wander aimlessly around until one of those humans find you, or be in a position to sustain your vampirism."

"Oh," she muttered.

"Dying by human hands isn't an honorable way for a vampire to die. I assure you that you can exist in this world and be protected by others of your kind. Will you take my hand?"

Falteringly, she placed her hand in his. The most amazing thing happened next. Her heart, which had stopped beating several days ago, pumped a few times as she touched him. She also felt...almost alive. Mikael's hand gripped her and led her away from the city. He moved with lighting speed, though the parking lots, the park, and further away through the edge of the city, beyond Berry Creek Falls.

Through the trees, Tara could make out a structure like a castle. That couldn't be. There weren't any such buildings in the area that she knew of. The building was too large to have gone unnoticed. Then again, she was finding out that anything was possible in the world she now belonged.

"We're home," Mikael stated.

He hadn't let go of her hand since she placed hers in his, and he led her though the double front doors and into the huge living room. The place looked like the inside of a regular mansion in a wealthy neighborhood.

"Don't worry. We are not alone," he grinned again and her heart pumped a few times.

"Sire," a man walked in, dressed in a suit. His skin was pale as a ghost with bloodshot eyes and sunken cheeks. If she wasn't yet turned, she might have been scared.

"George," Mikael, turned. "This is Miss Tara, prepare a suite for her, and gather those that are here, tell them I found her."

"Yes, Sire," the man retreated.

"Are you hungry?" Mikael inquired of her. "Let's see what we have inside the pantry."

"Yes, I'm hungry, but the only thing I seem to crave is human blood."

He led her through the living room and into another door leading off to the side. They passed by a kitchen which looked like it was recently used.

She chuckled at the thought of vampires cooking a meal. He led her into what appeared to be a cooling room, or a humongous refrigerator. There were shelves with perfectly cut steaks and bottles of red liquid.

"We'll remedy that," Mikael said. "That's normal, once you've tasted it. I'm glad you didn't harm that boy."

Tara looked at him peculiarly, "How do you know so much about me?"

"I heard your cry of anguish and I knew that it was the handiwork of the Enigma Thirst clan," he stated.

"The Enigma Thirst clan?"

"Yes, their thirst for human blood has no bounds," he picked up one of the glass bottles and walked to the kitchen.

Once there, Mikael pulled a tall glass from the cupboard and poured in the red juice. She could smell it and her mouth watered. He handed it to her and she took it. It tasted different from the boy's blood, but delicious just the same.

"What is it?" she asked after taking a couple of gulps.

"Deer's blood," he replied. "We import those and we get pigs blood from the butchers."

"Do you not take human blood?" she asked.

"Yes, only by consent," he poured himself a glass of blood and drank it in one go, licking his lips.

Tara finished her drink and Mikael refilled her glass, leaving the bottle empty. She drank the second serving which made her feel full, with the thirst for human blood subsiding somewhat. While he talked about Leon's clan and how they'd been rivals for centuries, his eyes pulled her in. She had though that Leon was the most gorgeous man she'd ever seen, and boy, was she wrong.

Mikael had something that made you want to touch him. Tara had thought that, now that she was no longer human, her human feelings were gone. The fact that her heart no longer beat in her chest was proof that she could no longer feel. That was far from the truth. She could hardly concentrate on what the man in front of her was saying, because she wanted to touch him and him to touch her.

"Have you been listening?" she heard him break though her thoughts. He was standing in front of her, looking down at her with slitted eyes.

"I...I'm sorry," she apologized, lowering her eyes.

"He'll come back for you," he was saying.

"What? Why? He abandoned me!"

Mikael took a lock of her hair and brought it to his nose. Then, he ran a finger along her jawline. "Because you are something special. He will not be able to get the taste of you out of his mind."

"I don't understand," she shook her head.

"You, my dear, were destined to be queen," his green eyes flamed when he whispered the words.

He ran his thumb across her bottom lip and a ripple of excitement coursed through her. Was he going to kiss her? She wanted him to. How would his tongue feel entwined with her? She wondered. She would have to wait, because Mikael dropped his hand and walked away, beckoning her to follow.

They went back to the living room where about a number of his clansmen had gathered. They bowed as Mikael entered. He told them what happened to her and asked that they accept her into their clan. They all agreed. Mikael then told her that she would be initiated the following night, giving her time to make up her mind fully.

After the meeting, he led her away. She followed him up the stairs, watching his tight butt in his black leather pants. No man had ever made her feel so alive when she was human. She was amazed at how fast she felt attracted to Mikael. It was like a total shock to her psyche. One minute she wanted to end her existence, and the next, she was in his arms. Her heart had raced for the first time for a man. It hadn't raced for Jared, not for Leon, nor for any man she had dated. However, now that it was dead, it pumped twice in the last couple of hours for Mikael, the Alpha she'd just met.

He took her to her suite, across the hall from his, a large room with a four-poster canopy bed. The room was something out of the Victorian era. The drapes and bed linen were deep wine red with wooden floors covered with bear skin rugs. Large, dark, intricately carved furniture completed the ensemble with a window seat.

"This is unreal," she blurted out.

"Ha-ha," Mikael's deep laugh echoed in the room. "This is a room suited for the queen. I can be yours permanently, if you desire."

"You speak in riddles, what do you mean by that?"

He walked over to her and stood close, "I think you know what I mean. I can protect you…love you…I will never abandon you."

A lump rose to her throat as she listened to his voice wash over her. Even his deep thundering voice was making her weak. Was he hypnotizing her? How the hell could she feel so totally enthralled by someone so quickly? Was it a vampire thing? Tara stepped back and turned away. She'd liked Leon. There was no doubt about that. When he had held her in his arms, it felt good. However, she could not recall feeling weak or her heart racing. Their kisses were sweet and sensual but not toe curling. She wanted to kiss Mikael, more than anything, even if it was to compare.

He was walking away when she turned back around, "Wait!" she said, not sure why she stopped him. He turned and looked at her questioningly. "Kiss me."

"What?"

"You want me to be your queen, then I ask you to kiss me," she stated.

"Will a kiss make it clear for you?"

"Yes," she whispered.

"You know," he moved towards her and cupped her chin. "Once we kiss, you may never want me to stop. You know what they say…one kiss may lead to another…"

"Just kiss me already, you talk too much," she urged and closed her eyes.

The anticipation of waiting was killing her. Mikael took his sweet time, running his thumb along her jaw, along her hair and finally lowering his head….touching his lips to her cheek. The electric sensation of his lips on her cheek only heightened the needed to feel his lips on hers. When she could no longer stand it, she twined her arms around his neck and urged his lips towards hers. Immediately upon their lips touching, it was not just toe curling, but hair raising as well. Her entire body felt like it was caught in an electric storm.

Considerably taken by surprise, Tara dropped her hands and stepped back. Her eyes were wide with shock as she stared at Mikael. He green eyes were molten and with flecks of orange embers. Her heart thudded loudly once more and she raised a hand to her chest. She was confused. Was this real or some sort of vampire induced sensation?

Mikael moved closer to her and grabbed her hand, placing it on his chest. "Do you feel that?" he asked as her hand felt the thundering under his rib cage. She shook her head. "It doesn't happen to everyone, human or undead, but when it does, it's something special."

"Special?"

"Hmm," he bent and swept her off her feet, walking her to the bed.

Tara's excitement grew. It was now or never, she told herself as Mikael made the few strides to the bed. Then, he laid her gently down, lowered his head, and whispered against her lips, "Sleep tight."

He was gone before she could swallow her disappointment. She sat up on the bed and doubled her fist. He was such a tease, getting her all worked up for nothing. What was his game anyway? One minute he was asking her to be his queen, and the next, he was leaving her with her body all tingly.

CHAPTER SIX

Tara slept until nightfall the following day. She must have been drained from all that happened to her for the past week. Mikael was waiting for her downstairs when she went down. Her mind was clearer now and she was curious to know how she could survive being a vampire. She had many questions which she wanted to ask Mikael.

"Have you rested well?" He asked as she descended the stairs.

"Yes, thank you. I'm hungry though," she replied with a shy smile.

"Come, let's eat," Mikael beckoned her to follow him to the dining area.

The table was set for a meal. This surprised Tara since she had assumed that vampires don't eat. She'd tried eating normal food, but it didn't sate her hunger. Quizzically, she sat at the chair offered to her, directly across from her host. He looked scrumptious to her. She had to give herself a mental thwack to concentrate on what was going on.

George was serving. First, he brought out a small bowl of blood for starter. Tara watched as Mikael took his soup spoon, scooped the red liquid, and brought it to his sensuous lips. Another naughty thought crossed her mind, of him devouring her breasts with them. She mimicked him by having the 'soup', which was light and airy. She wondered what it was.

"It's rabbit's blood," he raised his eyes and looked at her.

"Thanks," she looked away embarrassed, thinking that he may have guessed what she had been thinking earlier.

The next course was a very nice strip steak. With that, George poured them a glass of 'wine'. It was much richer and darker than the blood he'd served before, and without tasting it, she could not determine what it was. She had no idea that vampires dined this way, but looking at the meat before her made her suddenly very ravenous. The first bite was scrumptious. The drink was different from the one she'd had before but better.

"What is it?" she asked her companion.

"That's pig's blood. It's very rich. That's why it's so good."

"Wow, I can get used to this."

After the meal, Mikael took her for a walk, moving swiftly along the path they'd arrived at. She had to double her speed to catch up. It took some time before she realized that he was showing her one of the abilities of their kind. She also realized that she could see very clearly in the dark and was able to avoid many obstacles such as fallen trees. Being out like this made her see things differently. The past week was about her pain and denial. Now, she had a choice to live in the underworld, yet still, she was unsure.

"Now, I know that you are a mess inside your head, especially in the city," they had reached the city. He'd taken her on top of the building she jumped from the night before. "Look all around you," he said, stepping up behind her and putting his hands of her shoulders. "Now, close your eyes and inhale deeply," he instructed.

She complied, but it was too much. There were a jumble of different odors that made her feel overwhelmed. "No, I can't!" she protested.

"You have to filter them. What you are experiencing is a heightened sense of smell. This will keep you safe," he whispered in her ear, his lips brushing her skin.

A shiver went down her spine at the contact and she moved away from him in order to concentrate. Tara closed her eyes and inhaled deeply, absorbing each scent. It was scary but she did it several times until she was able to differentiate the difference between vampires, humans, and animals' scents.

"I did it," she breathed.

"Very soon, you'll feel like you've been this way forever. You will even come to think that you were meant to be this way."

"You think so?" she asked, uncertain.

He moved up behind her again, this time his body close to hers. He placed his large hands on her shoulders much like before, his stature towering her by nearly two feet. Mikael lowered his head and leveled his with hers.

"You, my dear, were destined to be a vampire queen," he murmured, then kissed her neck in the exact spot where Leon had bitten.

It was too much for her. Her knees gave out and she sagged back against him. She could feel his powerful body brace hers, his cock's impression was evident on her back. Oh how she wished she had the courage to seduce him, because she wanted to feel his lips on hers not on her neck. She wanted those hands to caress her skin. However, Mikael remained every bit the gentleman and made no move to make her his. She could tell he wanted her as much as she wanted him, but still, he held back. Why?

That question was left unanswered because her next lesson was watching what happens to vampires when they leave their clan or are left to fend for themselves. Tara was reminded of what parents did to teens who showed signs of wanting to do drugs or alcohol. They'd take them to the hospital where patients were dying of lung cancer or liver and kidney failure.

She saw rogue vampires feeding off animals and humans alike. He took her beyond Cupertino on the outskirts of San Jose to an area that was similar to a ghetto. The place seemed desolate, like a ghost town. There were sounds coming from seemingly empty buildings, like wailing.

"Ayeeeeeeeeeeeeeee!" a screamed pierced the night air, startling her.

A movement behind her caused her to grab at Mikael's arm. She didn't see anything, but whatever it was moved again, at lightning speed.

"Focus," Mikael commanded, his voice quite stern. "Stay still and don't be afraid."

Tara left out a long breath. She stood still, as she was told, and cleared her mind. Finally, she was able to see what was moving around them. It had raggedy white hair, with a face like a dried out corpse. Its teeth were long and discolored, and its bony body was covered with dirty rags.

"What is it?" she asked hoarsely.

"That was once a vampire maiden, just like you."

There were others like that around, from children to adults, even animals. "Why did you take me here?" she asked.

"I wanted you to know everything there is to know about our world. My clan will make sure this never happens to you."

Tara was curious about what she saw, "Did these beings belong to a clan?"

"Some, yes, but most of them were abandoned," he replied.

"Then, why didn't you help them?"

"We don't take anyone by force. You have to be willing to join our clan."

"Get me out of here," she urged.

When they were back in Mikael's residence, she had to ask him why the creatures she saw became that way. He told her that they mutated from feeding on bad human blood. He further explained that evil humans had bad blood that could cause a vampire to go rogue. That is the reason why the blood of the innocent was so valuable.

"It's sweeter. Evil blood is bitter," he said.

Blood of junkies, alcoholics, and those with diseases were sour and bad for you as well. Tara was amazed that every human's blood had a different taste. She learned that female blood was different from that of the male specie and that women who were sexually experienced were spicy, but easily forgotten. Sweet, innocent blood was the most sought after, and though she was turned, she was still a valuable asset and may not be safe.

After a long night of lessons, the night was finally over and the morning sun began to peep over the horizon, casting a golden glow over the city. It was time to get some sleep, but Tara hated being apart from Mikael. She felt herself torn as she headed up the stairs behind him, knowing that he would retreat to his chambers and her across the hall.

When they reached her room door, he stopped and turned to face her. She almost bumped into him for not watching where she was going. To Tara's surprise, Mikael pulled her gently into his arms and held her, stroking her hair lovingly.

"See you later," she heard his voice rumble in his chest.

Her cheeks pressed against his torso. "Later."

CHAPTER SEVEN

She stretched languorously, feeling refreshed for the first time in days. The soft, satin, baby blue nightgown, one of the many things Mikael had given her, rubbed blissfully against her skin. The morning sun peeped through the glass window casting a glow on her face. She opened her eyes and met Mikael's gaze. She stared at him a few seconds before her eyes travelled over his body. He was dressed in a black silk robe that left a lot to the imagination, standing a few feet from the bed. His powerful thighs stood slightly apart and she could make out his cock imprinted against the fabric. Her heart skipped a beat.

It was two weeks since she'd come into his lair. Two weeks of her wanting him to make love to her. Two weeks of him maintaining his cool and she was tired of it. Now, he was standing in her room with his eyes ablaze staring at the breast that had become exposed due to the strap of the nightgown coming undone.

"Good morning," he crooned.

"Good morning," she croaked, her eyes never leaving his middle section.

With the bulge beneath his robe, she wondered what it would look like. She'd seen naked men before, but this Vampire Alpha was more than seven feet, she was sure. He was like something out of a comic book. His arms were larger than her thighs, so she supposed his cock would be huge as well.

He folded his arms and watched her. "How are you feeling?" he asked.

"Better, almost normal."

"What have you decided?" he further inquired.

"About?"

"Will you be a part of this clan? There is no turning back," he warned. "Will you be my queen?"

She swallowed and stared at his thighs. They were like tree trunks against the black shiny cloth of the robe. "Yes," her voice was barely audible, but she was shaking her head to confirm.

He walked to the bed and sat, brushing the back of hand along her cheek. She liked his touch. Without saying anything, Mikael got in the bed beside her and engulfed her in his robust arms, pulling her against his solid frame. Her breasts pressed into his chest with the nipples hardening upon contact. As she wrapped her legs around his muscled thighs and snuggled closer, enjoying the thrill of his body next to hers, she felt his bulge.

"There is no turning back," he whispered against her hair.

"I know," she whispered back.

He began nibbling her neck, gently kissing her wound, the one Leon had left behind. A ripple of pleasure ran up and down her spine at the contact of his lips. Finally, his lips found hers and urged them apart. The kiss she'd waited for and dreamed about all night was happening. He sought out her tongue and entwined it with his, stroking it in an ardent caress.

She groaned at the thrill of it, wanting it not to end. Mikael's hand came up and cupped a breast, squeezing it gently and increasing the fire that started in the pit of her stomach. Boldly, Tara pulled the nightgown over hear head, exposing her body to Mikael. This was new to her, this bold new woman she'd become. She thought, maybe being a vampire isn't so bad after all.

Mikael took one nipple between his lips and suckled on it before going for the other, in the meantime rubbing his thumb over the one that's free. They stood erect as if they were meant specifically for his touch…and perhaps they were. His large hands enveloped each mount perfectly. She never thought her breasts were small. As a matter of fact, she was told several times that she was well endowed in that department. But Mikael's hands were so big that they fitted perfectly in his palms.

Leaving her breast, his hand ran along her belly and found its way to her thighs. There, he wedged his fingers between the garment and her skin and worked his way down to her vagina. She willingly parted her thighs to meet his touch. She wanted to feel his hands everywhere. Her fear of her first time had disappeared. All she wanted was to be taken completely.

"Make me your queen Mikael," she said, her lips brushing the skin of his chest.

To prove she was serious, Tara plastered kisses all over his chest, trailing her hot lips along his torso down to his navel. As she kissed his hard muscles, she heard his heart thud heavily. She followed her lips with her smooth hands, feeling every crevice and plateau. When she reached his waist, she pulled the string of his robe. The cloth separated, revealing what she'd imagined. Her breath caught at the sight and she gasped.

Bravely, she reached out and touched it. The thing bounced at her touch and she did it again. His shaft was rounded at the tip, with large veins bulging from it. She felt the bumps rub her palm when she ran her hand along its length. Mikael, seemingly impatient, pushed her back against the covers and wrangled his arms from the robe. He then pulled away her flimsy underwear and tossed it across the room.

Parting her thighs, Mikael, buried his face in the golden hair at her junction, before pulling apart her folds with his thumbs. With his tongue, he licked the opening of her chasm. A shot of electrical current ran through her. He did it again, this time lingering on her clitoris, before plunging his large tongue deeply into her flesh. He worked his tongue in and out of her, making her wetness ooze on his mouth. As if that wasn't enough, he added his middle finger to the assault, thrusting both tongue and digit into her at the same time, creating excruciating fiery explosions inside her.

She wriggled, gripping the bed clothing tightly, trying to control her body, while ripples of current ran through her. Mikael paused, only to cover her body with his, capturing her lips in the process. Tara could taste herself on him and it only served to heighten her pleasure. She wrapped her legs around his and felt him position his cock, pushing his hips forward, driving into her.

Surprisingly, there was only minor discomfort which disappeared after a few seconds. As Mikael moved his hips, she also moved hers. Maybe it was instinct, she didn't know. All Tara knew was that it felt like heaven. Their movements matched each other, with him gliding in and out of her. It felt natural. A dance that started slow gradually picked up tempo, his cock massaging her insides sending shards of fiery sparks, igniting her very core.

Gradually, the rhythm built, increasing speed. Two bodies dancing to the beat of their own music. The beating of their hearts fused together to create an explosion that brought them both to heights of ecstasy. Together, they exploded in rapturous bliss.

* * * *

They were locked in an embrace a few hours later, with Mikael nibbling the corner of her lips when his head suddenly shot up.

"What's the matter?" she asked.

He sighed and looked into her eyes, "The battle begins. Now, you must choose."

"Why do you always speak in riddles?"

"He's coming for you," Mikael stated, rising from the bed and pulling on his robe.

His magnificence was as breathtaking as a beautiful sunset. Tara could not look away from him, but his words stuck with her. Leon was on his way to get her. That bastard thought she belonged to him. How could he think she would want to go with him?

"What happens if I refuse to go?"

"Then, we fight to claim you. The winner takes you as their queen," he informed her.

"I thought I was your queen?" she sat up on the bed, her breast jiggling from the movement.

"Not yet, my sweet. You haven't been officially initiated into the clan. You haven't met the all of the clan. Come, we meet them now."

"What? Now?"

"Yes, get some clothes on," he waved his hand and the closet door opened, revealing a closet full of women's clothes.

How'd he do that? Tara's mouth fell open. The things she was learning about being a vampire were getting weirder and weirder. The super speed and supernatural powers she hadn't quite gotten used to yet. She pushed herself from the bed and walked to the closet, running her hands over the many items she had to choose from. When she turned, Mikael was gone. She ran to the bathroom and freshened up, then changed into a long white chiffon dress.

On the bureau was full of makeup and accessories. She walked over and picked up a golden hair brush which sat beside a rectangular box, brushing her hair until it shimmered. She then picked up a scarlet lipstick and ran it over her pale lips, bringing color to her face. As she looked at her reflection, she noticed she wasn't as ashen as before, and the wound on her neck had healed. Her skin was as white as porcelain and her eyes glinted

55

flecks of light.

Curiosity made her open the box, thinking it was some sort of jewelry. Inside was a silver dagger, about six in length. She bit her lip and picked it up, knowing well what the purpose of such a weapon was for. A small note in the box told her that this was her protection, a gift from the clan. Tara replaced the dagger and closed the box with a smile.

All that was left for Tara to do now was accept her fate, fully. She closed her eyes and pulled in a long breath. "I am a vampire, that's who I am," she said softly. "I am a vampire, that's who I am," she repeated much louder. "I am a vampire, that's who I am!" This time she shouted it and the window flew open, letting in a rush of air. Her eyes glinted and flecks of orange flamed in them. She could smell Leon coming, along with some of his clan, including Charlie.

Something else happened to her in that moment. She could hear Mikael's voice speak to her, in her mind, yet he was not in the room. She closed her eyes and listened. He told her not be afraid, that he would support any decision she made.

"If I go to Leon, would that prevent this war you talk about?" she asked.

"Perhaps, then he would have no reason to wage a battle against our clan," he replied. "Your decision should not be based on that. Your decision should be based on what it is you want. Come down. Let's meet the rest of the clan."

She was almost at the door when she returned and pulled out several drawers in the bureau. "There must be one somewhere," she muttered.

Finally, after messing up the entire room, she found red garter with a sheathe that she strapped to her thigh and placed the dagger securely in it. There was doubt that she would actually get to use it, but if there was going to be some sort of battle, she was better off prepared. She was downstairs in less than thirty seconds. She liked the speed at which she moved. When she arrived in what appeared to be a meeting hall, there were a few dozen vampires waiting for her, including the ones she met before. Leon was seated in a high back velvet chair on a podium and all eyes turned to her.

"Leon, the leader of the Enigma Thirst is on his way to claim Tara," he addressed the group.

"Didn't he abandon her and leave her for dead?" one from the group asked.

"Yes, he did. And that is why we should not let him take her."

"Why does he want her?" another asked.

Mikael looked at her, "Because she has the blood of a queen."

"Then, we should make her our queen," the man suggested.

"It is up to Tara. We would never take her by force. She has to choose," he stood and walked up to her. "It's your choice."

She could sense that Leon was outside the building with more like him. They were waiting for her. She moved towards the entrance with the clan behind her. She stepped out into the open. Mikael stood to her right with his legs apart as if ready for war and Leon on her left. He had a grim look, anger etched on his features.

A gust of wind blew the dried leaves, making them swirl in a circle. Her white dress flapped around her body defining her curves. She saw the flame alit in Leon's eyes. She looked across at the man she'd come to trust and saw his molten pools. Her long golden hair lifted behind her, flying in the wind, exposing her oval face with soft cheeks and scarlet colored lips.

This was hard. She'd thought it would be easy. If she went with Leon, she could avoid a war, but staying with Mikael would mean that Leon would cause trouble. She had no intention of causing trouble between the clans, especially one she just got acquainted with. She felt the right thing to do was avoid this war at all cost, even if it meant sacrificing herself.

"No!" she heard Mikael say. His lips hadn't moved, so it meant he was speaking to her telepathically. "Is that what you want, to go with Leon?"

She looked across at him and then moved, hearing Leon shuffle behind her. When she was within touching distance, she lifted a hand and touched Mikael's face. She trailed a long nail along his jawline, much the same way he'd lovingly caressed her before. Her heart moved, as always when he was near.

"I don't want to cause a war. I think I have fallen in love with you and this is my sacrifice for this love," she turned and shifted over to Leon, looking him straight in the eye. "I will come with you, but I will never be with you. You will never make my heart feel alive."

He gripped her by the hand and moved through the trees with his clan right behind. She knew Mikael loved her, even if they only knew each other less than a month. Their love was strong and maybe, she would find a way to set herself free.

Leon took her to a hideout underground, below the club. "You belong to me now." He grinned.

"I will never belong to you. You may have made me like this, but I will never willingly give myself to you."

"We'll see about that," he walked over to her and lifted a hand to touch her face, which she turned away. "We'll see."

"What made you want me back?" she asked sweetly. "You ignored me the night I came looking for you for help."

"You came to me, when?" he asked.

"After you left me in the park. I had a lot to deal with and needed you. You had some girl in your arms,' she spat at him.

"That was you? I didn't recognize you Tara," he said, taking a lock of her hair and sniffing it. "Had I known it was you, I would never have let you go."

"How can an Alpha not sense me?"

58

"It happens sometimes," he replied. "I think I had some bad blood recently. The night I was with you and the night you came to find me."

"Why now...why me?"

"Because you have the blood of the pure. Never been touched. I cannot get the taste from my tongue. Of all the women in the city, you are the most special."

"Ha ha ha," she laughed derisively at his comment. "Oh my, ha ha. So, that's why you came looking for me? Because I'm a virgin?"

"Yes, I should never have left you, but when you tasted my blood, you just passed out. I thought perhaps you were dead. I couldn't feel your life force anymore," he told her. "It was strange. That never happened before."

"You gave me your blood?" she didn't remember that.

"Yes, during our last kiss."

She remembered him kissing her just before she passed out. The kiss had tasted funny. That was it, the taste of blood. It didn't matter now anyway. He'd left her there. If he'd cared about her, he would have taken her with him and made plans to bury her if she was dead. He just left her body in the park, just like that. He didn't love her. She was just a possession to him.

"I have news for you, Leon," she walked up to him and looked into his eyes. "I already gave away what you so desire."

"What are you saying?"

She crooked her finger and beckoned for him to lower his head, where she whispered, "I am no longer a virgin."

Before he could reply, she sensed they were not alone. The club was surrounded by Mikael and his men. They had decided to fight for her, knowing that she'd made the choice to save them.

"It seems there will be a battle after all. It will be my pleasure taking down that arrogant bastard Mikael once and for all," Leon grinned.

CHAPTER EIGHT

They met at a clearing near the Berry Creek falls. Briefly, Tara wondered what would happen if she walked away from both clans and lived her life as an independent. Would that stop the pending battle between the two factions? It seemed not. Leon was angry that Mikael had bedded her first. Mikael on the other hand was fighting for his queen. The war was inevitable.

With no fighting skills before her change, Tara was depending on her pure vampire instincts to help her clan win. She watched as Leon and Mikael came face to face. Both powerful men flying in mid-air in ninja style martial arts. Before long, other clansmen were doing the same.

"If he wasn't my brother, I'd certainly slap him silly," someone moved up beside her.

It was Charlie looking on and shaking her head. "Aren't you going to fight me?" Tara asked, mentally preparing herself for the battle.

"Why? The one who turned me also abandoned me. That's why my brother became a vampire, to take revenge on him."

"What? You weren't always like this?"

"No. It was two centuries ago, the Silver Lights clan ruled. The Alpha's son and I dated for a while, but when he realized I was not a virgin, he was angry and rejected me, leaving me in a ditch to die."

"So, Leon willingly turned into a vampire to take his revenge?"

"Yes, he allowed me to turn him, then he found the boy and pierced his heart with a silver dagger."

"He is you real brother from the same parents?" Tara asked.

"Yes, our parents died when we were little, so all we had was each other. I'm sorry he did that to you. I tried to warm him to take care of you, but I think he had some bad blood during the day. Bad blood can make you do weird things," Charlie told her.

"How?" Tara jumped as Mikael and Leon tumbled to the ground in a tangled mess.

"It makes you feel drunk, like how alcohol distorts the human thought process," Charlie chuckled, looking at Mikael pinning Leon to the ground.

A sound zinged through the air and a stone landed in the center of Charlie's forehead, throwing her off balance. She was out a few seconds, but when she arose, she took on a grim look. Tara didn't even see the quiver on her back and the crossbow straps across her chest. She'd been so busy watching the Alphas fight, she failed to see what was happening around her.

Charlie placed an arrow in the bow and aimed it, shooting it into the shoulders of one of Mikael's men. The vampire pulled the arrow out with a howl, some flesh pulling out with the tip, blood oozing from the wound. He lunged at Charlie who aimed once more, the arrow piercing his side.

There was clanging of metal together as well. Tara looked around at the chaos she'd tried to avoid. The clanging she heard were swords. Mikael and Leon were still fighting hand to hand combat. She couldn't tell which clan was winning or losing. Eventually, she had to defend herself as she got caught in a fight. Actually, she wasn't even sure who the female vampire was that attacked her.

Raising herself off the ground came as naturally to her as breathing. With her determination to win, she grew stronger and could do anything she set her mind to. She caught a handful of white hair and pulled back the head of the owner, then landed her fist square between the eyes. Another fist caught the female's throat and she coughed loudly. Tara let her go, raised herself off the ground, and finished her off with a firm heel on her chin. Her opponent sagged to the ground.

Mikael and Leon were on the ground as well. They wrestled for a while and then Mikael extended his fangs and sank them into Leon's neck. Leon screamed and flapped his feet.

"What's happening?" Tara shrieked.

All the other clansmen stopped fighting to look on with interest. Mikael raised himself up, leaving Leon to look on with anger blazing in his eyes. "You scoundrel!" Leon roared, staggering to his feet. Someone threw Leon a sword, and he held it, pointing at Mikael. "Someone give this fool a sword," he ordered.

"Are you sure about this?" Mikael asked.

"Stop wasting time and take a sword."

One of the beta leaders of Mikael's clan handed him his sword. It had a sapphire in the middle of the pommel, with strange markings on the blade and quillion. Mikael gripped it and stood, legs apart, head down and waited. Leon lunged. Mikael sidestepped without using his sword. This angered Leon and he swiped the weapon, aiming for Mikael's neck, but the huge fellow bent backwards like a willow tree in the wind. He sprang back up as if he was on springs and flashed his blade. Leon looked down on himself. For a while there was nothing, then his white silk shirt started turning red.

Leon tore off the shirt and flung it on the dry leaves. Tara stood speechless as she witnessed what appeared to be a gash gradually close and disappear. Mikael had told her that vampires who fed on human blood healed easily. This was the first time she was witnessing this. It took her nearly three weeks to heal from the wound he gave her. It was simple. He made it a habit of feeding from human blood. She wondered how many young women he'd turned and abandoned. How many people were roaming the city because of Leon's thirst?

The two leaders went at it again, the clanking of their swords echoing through the green beyond the creek and waterfall. Beams of late afternoon sunlight peeping through the trees glinted off the blades as they zipped through the air. With a thrust and a twist of his wrist, Mikael's sword dislodged Leon's from his grasp, sending it flying through the air. It landed between the men, sticking up from the ground. Mikael brought the tip of his sword to Leon's neck and held it there.

"It's over," he stated.

"Do it," Leon urged. "Behead me now, or I won't let this go."

"It's over," Mikael reiterated. "Let it go, Leon. Tara has chosen."

Leon turned and looked across at Tara who was standing about three feet away. He pulled his sword, and in a flash, he was behind her, holding the sword to her neck. "It's not over. Tara comes with me."

"No Leon, you can't force her. That's not what the vampirism laws say," it was Charlie who spoke.

"Shut up, Charlie, you are no different from them. You think like a human. We are not humans. We are free agents. There are no rules in the underworld!"

Tara had to think fast because Mikael had a deadly gleam in his eyes and she was afraid that things would get worse. "I'll come with you!" She shouted for all to hear. "No more fighting. I'll go willingly, so stop this!"

While the men had been dueling and there was chaos around her, Tara had unsheathed her dagger, holding it tightly in her hand, palm down. She knew she could not be with Leon, not while her heart belonged to Mikael. There was only one thing to do and that was make him believe he'd won.

"Now Leon, drop your sword, or I shall be forced to let you behead me," she said to him in a calm tone.

He dropped the sword with a thud to the earth. She looked directly into Mikael's eyes and tried to communicate with him what she was thinking. She could see the disapproval of her plan in his face, but she could not let the blood thirsty Leon be her mate. She would rather die. She turned to face him and tipped on her toes, landing a kiss on his cheek. With precision borne of determination, she quickly brought up her hand and shoved the blade of the dagger into his chest.

At first, he looked at her disbelievingly, then what seemed like pain twisted his features, before he went blank. The alpha leader clutched his chest where the silver dagger stuck out. There was blood oozing from the wound. No one rushed to his aid, even his sister Charlie looked on with disinterest. He sank to the earth near his sword as the color of his eyes slowly faded. Soon, he would fade as well, being swallowed up by the earth.

Tara stepped back, backing into a brick wall with hands that enclosed her in a tight embrace. "What have you done?" Mikael uttered.

"I'm sorry," she whispered. "I'm sorry!" her voice rose a little.

"No need to be sorry," he crooned. "Now, you will be feared by all the clans in the underworld."

CHAPTER NINE

"So that's it?" Tara asked Mikael. She thought there would be some backlash for taking out Leon.

"Hmm," he murmured, trying to kiss her, but she wriggled from his grasp and walked to the edge of the waterfall.

They were at the large rock where the water flowed over into the creek. They could see the city light flicker from afar. The night seemed peaceful, and for the first time in a month, Tara felt normal. She felt more normal than before she entered the world of vampirism.

"So, what happens to his clan now?" she questioned Mikael.

"Why are you talking so much? Don't you want to know what the final initiation is?"

That got Tara's attention, "What final initiation? I thought the clan did that last night after the battle."

He grinned, "I'm not talking about the clan initiation…I'm talking about the final rites to being my queen."

"Is there more?"

"Hmm," he was still grinning and looking her with orange flecks in his eyes said. "All you have to do is follow my lead."

"Okay," she giggled, allowing him to sweep her up in his arms and capturing her lips.

"I'm trying something new, so don't be afraid," he warned.

Tara's eye's widened when Mikael hovered in midair with her, then everything went distorted. She felt dizzy for a few second before she realized they were not in the forest but on top of a very tall building. This building was not in Cupertino, but rather on the Aon Center building in Los Angeles.

"How'd we get here?" she asked in awe.

"I've been experiencing this new ability recently, so I decided to try it with you."

He was still hovering with her. Once again, he took her lips. She twined her arms around his neck and pushed her breast into his chest. She adjusted herself to face him, since she was lying crosswise in his arms, in the process, wrapping her legs around his thick waist. Their kiss intensified with their tongues entwined. Tara's nipples were already hard and she felt that her dress was a hindrance to her need to feel Mikael's skin next to hers.

Still holding the kiss, she managed out of her dress which floated away across the city. She was now naked, in the arms of her clan prince, hovering over LA. Mikael broke away from her lips, only to devour her breasts. He moved from one to the other nipping and nibbling them as he pleased. She moaned with pleasure at the excitement that ran up her spine. Meanwhile, she helped him out of his shirt, and while he continued his assault on her breasts, she unbuckled his pants, allowing every piece of garment to be carried away by a slight breeze.

"This is a little strange," Tara breathed.

"Are you uncomfortable?"

"No, silly," she giggled against his lips. "I'm dying to know how it feels to make love above the city."

With her legs still wrapped around his waist, Tara wiggled until she felt his shaft touching her honey pot. Another adjustment had the tip pushing into her already wet area. She was worried that any vigorous movement might cause them to fall, but then again, they couldn't really get hurt, could they? Another twist of her hips had Mikael's huge cock sliding into her, filling her to the hilt.

Her clitoris touched the base of his pelvis tantalizingly. She shimmied and the love button brushed his him. The feeling was more profound than she'd anticipated and she did it again. She could feel every bump on his cock rubbing her walls with each movement of her hips. She continued by moving her hips up and down causing his dick to slide in and out of her.

"This is awesome!" she screamed. The pleasure of their coitus coupled with the thrill of being on top of the world was a little too intense. Soon, her walls were throbbing as she felt the dam within her broke, "No, nooooo," Tara screamed, trying to stop herself but it was too late.

Her disappointment made her feel like she wanted to bawl. So, this is how men with premature ejaculation felt, she thought. However, Mikael wasn't done yet. In warp speed, they were back at the creek, just below where they were standing earlier.

"Now, let's do this properly," Mikael said, placing her gently on the dried leaves on the ground.

His lips began making their way from her lips to her neck, where he stopped to sniff her. Using his tongue, he made a path down to her breasts, taking the time to lick their tips until they were standing as erect as his cock was. Very soon, he was kissing and nibbling the flesh below her navel, then trailing his tongue towards the slit betwixt her thighs.

He wedged her thighs apart and parted her flesh, sticking out his tongue and making one long swiping motion along her opening. He did so several times, each time making sure to let his tongue linger on the tip of her clitoris. Using his index finger, Mikael plunged into her and began moving it back and forth. His finger fucking and licking her clitoris was arousing her all over again…or perhaps she was quite fulfilled, she couldn't tell. This need was even more intense than before, and she ached to complete what they had started.

Tara also wanted to lick his cock like a candy, to taste it and feel it in her mouth. She wrangled herself from his grip on her hips and sat up straight. Mikael looked at her questioningly. His question would soon be answered when she gripped his shaft and told him to lie back. Before she could accomplish her task, Mikael cupped her face and pulled her to him, covering her mouth with his.

She broke the kiss to center her attention on his cock, first kissing it all over, feeling it throb beneath her lips. From the root of it, she ran her tongue along its length, then she circled the ridge with her tongue's tip. She felt Mikael tense and a guttural sound escaped him. This gave her encouragement to continue her exploration. She cupped his testicles in her palms and jiggled them, wanting to know what they felt like. When she did that, his cock bounced. This amused her and excited her at the same time.

Wanting to know what would happen next, she licked his balls, then taking them in her mouth and sucking gently. Mikael arched his back and let out a yelp.

"Did that hurt?' she asked, anxious that she may have gone too far.

"No," his voice was strained. "No, it doesn't hurt...at all."

She kissed his balls and continued to lick it gently, while Mikael rubbed his thumbs on both her nipples. With careful attention, Tara closed her lips around the head of Mikael's penis and suck delicately. Afterwards, she slowly took him in, but she was only able to go halfway because of the thickness of it. However, she moved her golden head up and down, making sucking noises, feeling him bulge in her mouth. Then, before she could complete her mission, Mikael gripped her shoulders and urged her up. He brought her to settle astride him. He then reached between then gripped her hips, eased her up, and settled her on his hard standing cock.

Tara heard him sucking his breath as she slid down his pole. It stretched her to the maximum as her cunt tightened around him. Methodically, she moved up and down, her slippery flesh moving over his cock sweetly. Gradually, the tension built between them, intensifying her rhythm. Her breasts agitated furiously with her wild seesaw pattern.

She knew her time was near again when Mikael pressed his thumb to her clit. Was he doing it deliberately to make her come? She believed so, because his face was twisted as if in pain and he was grunting loudly. She increased the tempo and leaned into his thumb, allowing her clit to feel the slight pressure he was putting on. Then, all of a sudden, she felt like she was bursting in flames as her epicenter exploded with heat.

An earsplitting cry erupted from her as she completed her orgasm. It shook her core and she twitched violently, tightening her body around Mikael. He curled upward, pushing his pelvis up. His eyes rolled back, his teeth ground together in the act of trying to contain his explosion. There was no containing it. A bellow, like a lion in pain, escaped him, rumbling over the hills and perhaps echoing through the city with its thundering sound.

That was when she realized what she must do. Tara's fangs had extracted and her eyes became orange flames in a fire pit. She sank her fangs into Mikael's soft shoulder and licked the blood as it oozed from him. It was the best taste she'd ever had. When she was done, she ran her nail along her breast, only just cutting the soft flesh. As the blood trickled down her still jiggling mound, his long tongue reached out and lapped it up, licking her wound dry.

Mikael looked up at Tara with mirth written on his face, "Now, you are my queen."

THE END

Can't get enough romance?

See the next page for a sample chapter of Book 2 of the series!

Alphas of the Underworld:

Heart of the Vampire Queen

By Milena Fenmore

CHAPTER ONE

How do vampires mourn? One will never quite know. For Charlie, whose heart had stopped beating when she became a vampire some one hundred years ago, she felt an emptiness in the pit of her stomach. She missed her brother, Leon; his laugh, his womanizing ways, and his over protectiveness of her. That was the extent of her grief.

She closed her eyes and inhaled deeply, still sensing his presence, like a ghost. Yet, once a vampire dies, that was it. There were no ghosts, no reincarnation, nothing. Vampires were not living souls, yet they were not dead, and that is why they were known as the undead. Charlie thought that undead was an unfair name since many vampires experience human emotions such as love, hate, ecstasy, passion, and to some extent, pain. She fingered her crystal amulet which hung on a black string at her throat and wondered what it was like to feel love.

Now, there were decisions to make. Being next in line to be leader of her clan, she must give her answer by midnight. However, there was trouble brewing as there were talks of revenge for Leon's death. Charlie tapped her finger on the glass top desk in her office and squinted her indigo eyes. The Underground Club was now hers. She'd done most of the work running it while Leon wandered about the city of Cupertino chasing after innocent blood. Now that he was gone, she must continue with her work.

A part of her missed him because she loved her brother, but she was also angry that he'd created a mess and left it behind. The rules for any vampire clan was never to abandon someone you've turned. You must guide them and show them the way of a vampire, give them a choice to join the clan. The choice to go independent must be theirs.

The truth was that Leon abandoned Tara after she trusted him. He turned her and left her in a park to die. Then, after she was accepted into their rival clan, he suddenly realized she was destined to be queen and wanted her back. It was too late then. Tara had already fallen in love with Mikael, who rescued her, taught her true vampirism, and embraced her wholeheartedly.

Charlie glanced at the clock and saw it was near midnight. She pushed her chair back and stood. There was a clan meeting at midnight to hear her answer. Accepting the leadership position would be the only way to save her clan. There was no way they could win against a powerful vampire shifter like Mikael. She saw it that day, the day her brother died, the brief moment he almost was about to change. The man had great control over who he was…part vampire and part something else, something dangerous.

"Ryan," she called to the bartender as she reached the bar counter.

The place was buzzing with activity and the low drone of the metallic music was hypnotic. The lights were dim, as usual. There was a long bar stretching from one corner of the room to the next with two and four seater tables expertly set about the rest of the room.

"Yes, Boss," the tall thin bartender with titanium eyes looked up from his task.

"I'll be going now. You hold the fort and have Grace lock up," Charlie said in her usual husky tone.

Ryan swallowed. She could see his Adam's apple move up and down his throat. She liked the guy but he wasn't her type. She didn't know what her type was, but it wasn't her barkeep. She looked at him and smiled, knowing that she affected him. Ryan looked away, embarrassed. It amused her. If only he was human, he would have gone red.

"Yes, Boss," Ryan answered.

Charlie walked away, her red wavy hair falling midway down her back shimmered in the dim light of the club. When she entered the parking lot, she stopped. Something was amiss. She smelled blood that wasn't quite human. There was a hint of danger and she readied herself for whatever it was; however, the scent quickly disappeared.

She got in her car and drove to the mansion on the outskirts of Cupertino just at the edge of the Black Mountains. It was also close to the wild life sanctuary. The car was just for show as vampires didn't need transportation and was able to move at warp speed if needed. Living in a city full of humans and whatever else there was, she had to keep up appearances or risk exposing her clan.

She parked the car in the driveway and moved quickly, as silently as air into the living room of the home she and her brother owned. It wasn't a place Leon used a lot. He preferred the seclusion and darkness that the underground home he built under the club offered. She hated it there and much preferred the mansion. The great hall could easily hold three hundred and they were all gathered there waiting for her. There were about two hundred more of her clan scattered in the mountains, but they all could not be there for whatever reason.

"You're here," an elder pointed out.

"Yes, I'm here, Elder" she acknowledged.

Clonus, with white hair and black bloodshot eyes, moved closer. "What have you decided?"

"I will take my rightful place as queen, the way it was meant to be," she beamed.

"Then, let's prepare the ceremony!" he announced.

An altar with a golden goblet, a golden dagger with sapphire stones in the handle, and golden scepter matching the dagger were prepared in the center of the room. To the east wall where the group faced was the podium with her jeweled chair, just like a real queen. The seat, arms, and backrest of the chair were wrapped in scarlet velvet with rubies placed in the intricately carved head of the back. It was a work of art.

Each member of the clan was required to place a drop of their blood in the goblet using the dagger to pierce the hand. Afterwards, Charlie was asked to kneel before the elders of the clan.

"Today, we honor you, queen of the Enigma Thirst clan," Clonus stated. "But first, you must agree to uphold our sacred laws."

"Yes, Elder," Charlie responded.

"Then, do you agree to never kill a human unless your life is in danger, nor will you harm those from your own clan?"

"I agree."

Clonus continued, "You will not abandon a charge unless they wish to be independent. You will not abandon your clan for another, and you will not mate with any being from another clan."

"Yes, Elder, I agree."

"You may take a human mate, but the human must agree, with the full knowledge of what you are."

Charlie once again replied, "I agree."

"The most important rule of our clan is that you may never mate with a shifter being. You may only take a mate of our kind or a human mate. This rule cannot be broken. If you break this rule, you will face the possibility of being vanquished," the elder paused and looked at her. "Do you agree to uphold all these rules?"

"I agree," she replied in a loud clear tone.

The elder took the goblet and placed it at her lips. She drank the entire contents and licked her lips. Now, she had the blood from her clan running through her veins. The missing clan members would offer their blood to her at another meeting. She could sense each and every one of them. She could tell what they were thinking, and that very night, she would face her first challenge.

Clonus took the goblet and placed it on the altar, then picked up the scepter and placed it carefully in her outstretched hands. Charlie stood and looked among the crowd. There were those there that did not approve of her, but they could do nothing because this was her birthright. A hundred years ago, her brother formed this clan and the rule clearly states that the next in line to lead the clan would be of like blood.

"We will now commence our clan meeting," the elder announced. "On the agenda is the death of our beloved leader Leon."

"Why is that on the agenda? We already know how he died," Charlie was confused.

"Some of our people think that he met an unfair death and the Moonlight Hearts Clan should pay," the elder replied.

"You don't agree, do you?" she could see it in his eyes.

He hesitated and looked about the crowd. There was some tension in the room. "I think waging a war against Mikael and his clan would be sure annihilation for us," he stated only for her ears.

Charlie turned to face the crowd. Her eyes leveled with a tall fellow whose blood she could smell from a million miles away. He reeked of vengeance and bitterness, and she immediately knew he was the main instigator. She observed his black slicked back hair, his ashen skin, and black beady eyes. He's gone rogue, she thought.

"I see there is a division between us. Those in favor of war against the Moonlight Hearts, step forward," she instructed.

About fifty of her clansmen stepped forward while the others backed away. Charlie closed her eyes and inhaled deeply. She knew why they were determined to avenge her brother's death. They were changing, slowly but surely. Soon, they would be uncontrollable, turned into a cross between vampire and demon. These vampires were those who thirst for blood…any blood. The blood from junkies and outlaws were easy prey. That's why they were like this, they were ingesting bad blood that could make then into demons.

"Leon broke the vampire law. He turned a human against her will and then he left her to die," she looked from one face to another.

"Don't you want revenge? He was your brother by birth," said the rogue who stepped forward menacingly.

She ignored him and continued to speak, "Not only did he abandon her, he waged a war against Mikael and his people when he realized she was accepted by them, when he realized she was destined to be queen."

"Still, he should not have died by their hands. Mikael must pay," the rogue argued.

"If we go up against their clan, we face certain demise. Do you even know who Mikael is?" she stepped forward and faced him squarely.

He smelled of fresh kill. The kind that turned vampires into demons. His latest was a junkie. She could smell the drug-ridden blood on him and her nostrils burned from it.

"We will avenge our leader's death," he turned to his mob. "Won't we?"

"Aye," they chorused.

"As your queen, I cannot approve this. You will not go up against Mikael and his men," her voice took on a commanding tone.

"And what if we do?" he asked, his face twisting into ugliness.

"You will face certain destruction, and for disobedience, we will have you punished according to our law."

He made a step towards her, but Charlie stood her ground. "Then, we leave this godforsaken clan!"

Charlie was uncertain what to do, but she knew the eyes of the elders were upon her. Clansmen threatening to leave the clan was no simple matter. Was she doing the right thing opposing this war they wanted to wage? She chanced a glance at Clonus. She could hardly read his expression but she could sense his mood. He agreed with her decision.

"I will ask this once. Will you leave this clan?" she looked back at her protestors. "Step forward all who wish to disengage themselves from our people."

Charlie sensed there was uncertainty among some of them. About a dozen or so stepped back into the crowd while the rest stepped forward, including the rogue.

"Then leave your amulets here, lay them at my feet. When you leave this faction, you can never return. You will become rivals and you can never mate with one of ours," a few more stepped back after hearing that. "Most of all, you will become outcasts."

"The law says we can join any clan we choose!" the rogue shouted.

"The law also said that no clan will accept a half-demon. No clan will want your kind, it's too risky," she calmly stated, never taking her eyes off him.

One by one, each of the outcasts laid their amulet down at her feet. Charlie could see hostility, among other emotions, on their faces. Each amulet represented their sect and the protection offered by it. Without this amulet, they could do whatever they wanted without having to answer to anyone. They were free to live as they pleased; however, there was no protection from vampire hunters.

Under vampire law, they could form their own faction but they would be under the radar, constantly on the run because they were now known as outcasts and no longer considered a part of the treaty between vampires and humans. They would be feared and hunted, just because they had become "Rogues".

As the last amulet was placed at Charlie's feet, an elder, known as The Keeper, one of the oldest vampires to walk the face of the earth, came forward and collected them, and placed them in a protective box that only he could open. Every clan had a Keeper.

"Well done," Clonus said with a pleased expression. The others all nodded in agreement. "We knew of this league of rogues and what they stood for. This is not what this clan is about. We know that your brother formed this clan, but remember that many of these brothers here have been around for centuries. We came to this clan because our people were annihilated and we had no home."

"I know Elder. Even so, we must keep the vampiric laws or face destruction."

"Only a true queen puts her people before herself. I know this isn't easy for you, but you did well," Clonus looked around the room. "Hail our queen."

"Hail to our queen!" many of them shouted.

The meeting broke up and most of the vampires left the room, leaving only the elders and their new queen.

All of a sudden, Clonus asked, "When will you choose a mate?"

Charlie was surprised. She never thought of taking a mate, but now that she was queen, she supposed that she had to do something about that. "I will think about it, Elder," she replied.

"Very well then. You have one hundred days to choose," Clonus replied.

"Is that in the bylaws? How come a male can lead without a mate but I have to choose…," she replied frantically.

"Relax, we were just joking. There is no such law. You can choose a mate whenever you wish, my queen," Clonus laughed and so did a number of the others. "The look on your face was priceless though."

She laughed lightly at their joke knowing that they were trying to make her relax after the tension of a few minute before. This meant that the elders accepted her and those who opposed her were gone from their sect. It didn't make things easier because she knew they were going to cause trouble.

"My queen," another elder known as Mark interrupted. He looked quite serious and Charlie sensed there was trouble. "We have another issue on our hands."

"Please tell me," she encouraged.

"We have been challenged by a new faction," he stepped forward and all eyes were upon him. "A shifter gang." There was shuffling and murmuring among the group. There was a bit of unease.

"Are you sure about this?" she asked, but even as she questioned him, she knew it to be true.

He nodded, "Yes, my queen, it is so, and they are seeking blood."

"Why is that so?" she asked as an uneasy feeling settled over her.

Mark was quick to reply, "This mansion was originally their birth parents' home. He wants to reclaim what is rightfully theirs. The land and most of the mountain range was once theirs as well, but they were chased off by the shifter dogs."

"So, this is a shifter family?" she proceeded to ask.

"No, it's a community. They have grown their community with werewolves who've lost their homes or clan. It's quite a large faction, similar to ours."

"This isn't good" Charlie began to pace the clan hall. "Who is their leader?"

"His name is Greyson, but he hardly ever makes an appearance himself. His brother, Bryce, second in command, is the one who you will likely meet."

"Tell me more about this community of wolves," she sat in her high chair and listened as Mark addressed the group.

"As we all know, wolves are led by the eldest in the pack. This is not so with this group. The leader is chosen based on his lineage. But more so than that, he has the special skills of a fighter that no one else possesses. He is fearless...," Mark stopped and frowned. "He reminds me of Mikael, come to think of it."

Charlie looked at Mark, "So, you are saying that their clan operates like our clan?"

"Yes," Mark replied. "That's quite progressive. However, their patriarchs hold a council, much like our elders here, and they do the same as us when it comes to upholding the law of the pack." Mark stopped speaking and waited for her to tell them what to do.

There were fifteen elders in all and all eyes were upon her once more. Elders were seniors, who walked the earth long before the others. To become an elder, a vampire must be more than three centuries old. The elders know the secrets to survival and have defied death many times.

"My queen, they want to destroy us. These shifters are dangerous. They destroy anything in their path to gain territorial rights," Mark continued.

"Set up a meeting," Carlie instructed.

"What for?" one elder asked.

Clonus stood silently watching and she glanced his way. He was her rock. She could sense his emotions easily and knew when he approved or disproved of anything. Now, he waited for her to make her decision, and she knew he would go along with whatever she said.

"We need to coexist with every other being. If we wage war every time another faction moves in, we will become extinct in no time. We coexist with humans. We can do the same with other beings as well." Everyone nodded in agreement.

"Very well, we meet the shifters," the elder replied.

To be continued...

Grab your copy of Alphas of the Underworld: Heart of the Vampire Queen to find out what happens next!

Thanks a Billion for being such an awesome reader!

Here's our secret BONUS story just for you! Turn the page to start reading "Dragons of the Underworld: Betrothed to the Alpha Dragon" and keep the flame lit!

Dragons of the Underworld:
Betrothed to the Alpha Dragon

DAVINA BARON

PROLOGUE

Many years ago…

The time had finally come. He knew he could not wait or put it off any longer. He could feel the dragon inside of him fighting against him for the truth to be known. The dragon unfurled its wings and fanned the flames inside of his body as he clasped onto his betrothed. It was the moment of truth. The moment he told her what he really was. As terrifying as this moment was for him, it was something all dragons went through.

His father and some of his older brothers told him stories about the women they fell in love with and how they told them the truth for the first time. He was told the key to successfully revealing the secret was finding the one woman you were meant to be with, and she will not be afraid. He knew it was Addy. He loved her and he wanted to spend the rest of his life with her.

He gripped her tight, bending her slightly backwards before he pressed a hot, open-mouthed kiss on her lips. Around him, cheers rang out. Tomorrow was his wedding day, and he wouldn't go into it with any lies. That meant he had to tell her. Despite the bawdy cheers around him, he had to look to her father. He nodded before she would clasp his hand. He wrapped her in her cloak, fingers lingering on her soft skin, before he pressed a kiss to her forehead.

"Come now, lass. I have something you need to see." He spoke clearly enough. He knew his kin would be able to hear him, but this was what he needed to do.

Her giggles as they ran for the trees were contagious. He chuckled himself, her excitement wrapping around his heart. For a beast as dangerous as he was – she made him feel young and quiet of heart. There was no raging, no urge to harm those around him when he was near her. She tempered the flames that raged through his heart and strengthened him. She made him weak at the knees. She had since the day he met her. He stopped her there, pressing her against a tree as they neared the clearing where he released himself. He sank his fingers into her red hair, the silken strands a way for him to control her. Their open-mouthed kiss was full of heat and need. He had one more night before he could make her his completely.

"Adam, love. What do you want to show me?" Her hand was on his cheek. A heated touch, even though her skin was cooler than his. He nestled his whiskery beard into her hand before stepping away. He led her to a fallen tree, and made her sit down, his large hands encasing her slender shoulders.

"Whatever you do, Addy my love, don't scream and run, please." He was pleading with her before he stepped back. Stripping from his clothes was natural, and he saw the moment she spotted just how ready for her he was. Her cheeks flared red, a dusky color that made him want to lick them. But she looked. Even as he reached inside, and his other side exploded from him.

Huge, the dragon landed as delicately as he was able to. Large talons creased the ground as he exhaled steam. His scales, his armour wasn't just black. It was iridescent with a purple and blue sheen across scales, scored from a lifetime or tens of battles. She'd paled. He could see that without lowering his head. He was taller than three large men standing on top of each other's shoulders, but when he returned to his human frame, he was just taller than average, but muscled more than the average farmer or smithy.

Addy froze and her eyes grew wide as she saw this creature standing beside her. Was this Adam? Did her lover really just turn into a dragon before her eyes? It was obvious to Adam by the look on her face that she was both scared and confused. Adam knew he needed to say something quickly to soothe her. The last thing he ever wanted to do was scare her. He loved her.

"Shh, Addy lass. Tis only me, your Adam. You can't tell anyone about this, do you understand?" He crouched in front of her. His hands reached for hers, but she flinched away from him.

"Tell anyone? They'd lock me up! You are a monster. A creature…how could…how could I let you touch me?" He flinched back from her. His blue eyes brightened just a little as they filled with tears.

"But, Addy, lass, please -", she broke him off with a shake of her head. Her eyes were too bright, her cheeks spotted with colour. She held no interest in his body now. He could see.

"No, you beast! Get away from me." A broken sob came from the woman he loved. He wrapped his arms around his stomach as she ran away from him. She fled into the night and left him alone to roar his anguish.

***

Adam had no idea how long he spent sulking and agonizing over the way Addy had reacted to learning about his true self. The pain he felt deep in his chest was something he had not experienced before. She was his soul mate and dragons were not really individuals who fell in love with more than one person. When they fell in love – they fell in love hard. They were one of the most loyal creatures on the planet.

"Addy…" He whispered before standing up and brushing himself off. He had to find her, to talk to her. If he could just explain to her. If he could just see her one more time. He knew she would remember how she felt about him. He knew they could be happy together. He needed Addy to be ok with this.

That was the moment Adam decided to set out to find his love. He could remember the way she smelled and the way she tasted. He used this memory to track her down. He spent years of his life chasing down leads and following her smell. Never giving up on the love he had with her. Every time he would get close to where he knew she was – something happened and then she was gone again.

Years had passed. Adam had friends and family members who told him continuing to search for her was a waste of time. After all, she was a human. Even if he did find her, she would not be the same young and beautiful girl he fell in love with. She would have grown old by now. There was even a chance she could have passed away. He shook his head ignoring all the advice his friends and family had given him. If Addy was gone, why was it he could still smell her? He had to find her – he just had to. He knew they were right about her growing old and passing away, but since he could feel when she came back to the world, he knew reincarnation did indeed exist.

CHAPTER ONE

Addison Moore knew as soon as she backed into him that she was in trouble. She could feel every muscle, the hardness of him behind her. Her lips dried, and she run her tongue across them. Her skin crawled as she turned to face the man, an apology that soon faded as she was held captivated by brilliant blue eyes. The bar was crowded and the people surrounding them pushed them together as soon as she began to move again to the music. She was captivated.

He had hard eyes, but she felt like she knew him. She could feel the heat from his skin warming her as they danced. Then, it scalded her. She realised he was pale. That skin which should have held a tan was chalky, almost green looking. She knew him from somewhere. Her eyes narrowed as she flinched away a little. She was wary.

Something burned in the air. She could smell it. He ran his eyes over every inch of her flesh, but she didn't feel violated. She felt warmed. Heated by the touch of his eyes alone. If they could do this, what would his hands do?

She was caught in a half-remembered dream. Her mind stole her away to the dreams of heat, of kisses stolen and innocent laughter. Of brief touches that burned her. His hands clasping her shoulders halted her. His finger-tips brushed the sharp edges of her shoulder blades, his thumbs sliding up to her throat, stroking – caressing. She groaned lightly as he grabbed her hair, the russet red strands captive between his fingers. It was like she was transported to another place when he touched her, but she felt certain she'd never seen him before. It was impossible to know him. Still, she was drawn towards him.

She groaned again as he bent his head towards her. As he captivated her with his lips, to brush his cheeks against her own. To glide his lips from her collarbone up her throat. To press hot kisses with teeth to her jaw, to tug her ear with those same teeth. He grazed her flesh as they finally kissed. As he took her mouth and made it his own, she moaned, pressing herself against him. The stranger could kiss. He left her knees trembling. Her stomach churning as she relied on his strength to keep her on her feet. He spoke into her ear, a whisper filled with so much longing that her stomach churned.

"Finally, my Addy. I missed you so much…why'd you run from me?"

The question wasn't something she could answer. Instead, she tried to pull from him. She was panicking. This was finally too much. It was one thing to kiss a stranger in a crowded bar, but another for one to decide he knew her. He clutched at her as though she was keeping him from drowning. She needed to be free. Needed her own space. Her eyes narrowed a little before she hit his chest, before she struggled and tried to kick him.

"Let… go…. of…. me." Her voice was cool and determined. She wouldn't scream and cause a fuss. He was obviously disturbed in the head.

Something had to be wrong with him if he thought she was someone he knew. She was nothing to anyone. Her eyes closed a little. She was nothing any more. She'd lost the ones that mattered to her, about her. A groan filled her throat before the sound of two men fighting stole his attention. She could feel his grip sliding from her waist to her arms, and then to her hands. With a quick twist, a wriggle, she fled him. The crowd aided her as she ducked lower, ignoring the almost desperate cries he gave behind her. She felt guilty, it was true, but she wasn't going to be held responsible for some crazy man's delusions of who she actually was or wasn't.

It was just strange that she could still taste him on her lips, could still feel the heat of his touch on her. The scrape of calloused fingers on her throat. She knew he was a worker, a hard one at that. There was something about him that still kept her on edge. The knowledge in his eyes, a blue which seemed to pierce her, seemed to see right through to her soul. A groan slipped forth from between her lips as she wrapped her arms around her stomach and hurried off. She needed to stop thinking about him. He was just a crazy man who lost his way. So what if he smelled amazing and felt even better against her body.

Maybe the next woman he kissed would be the one he thought she was. That thought roused a burning lick of jealousy, though she didn't know why. He was nothing to her. She had to remember that. So what if that was the first time in years she'd felt something other than apathy. He was just a particularly good-looking crazy guy, and he made her feel more than anyone had in years. It was tough to convince herself of that though. Somehow, she felt like she knew him well. She made her way home after slipping through alleys and crossing streets, just in case he tried to follow her. She'd seen the desperation and need in his eyes. Felt it in the grip that was almost bruising. Knew it from his desperate calls when she finally walked away.

She was so stressed when she got home that she sought her bed. Her head was throbbing, breaking apart as she walked. These migraines accompanied night terrors, and she knew that she'd soon be insensible. And then inconsolable with the after-effects of her nightmares. The memories of her parents and younger siblings dying in the same crash she survived with only minor scarring. A few faint lines along her brow, against the hairline – and the nightmares. She hated it. Hated knowing she had no one to care if she survived or not.

The last thought she had as she laid her head down to sleep was that he'd known her name. How the hell had he known her name? That alone managed to terrify her enough for her dreams to begin in the worst way possible, with the sound of metal crunching and her ceaseless screams for her parents to answer her..

CHAPTER TWO

For centuries, he'd waited for her. He'd hunted for her. Every time he got close, it was too late. She fled him. Left him. Now, he was on alert. He'd followed her scent, his body aching, burning for her after the taste he'd had of her mouth. She was sweet and spicy. She was everything to him in that moment. The dragon hiding within him raked at him, flamed him, Burned him with the need to be closer to her. He stood outside her home, watching over her. No matter what he did, all he had on his mind was his Addy. Everything about her was the same. Adam knew it was her, from the green eyes and red hair to the porcelain skin that cooled his internal fires down.

She was everything he wanted in a mate. Even down to the fiery nature that had her fleeing from him. As if he'd let her get away again. He wanted her too much for that. He needed her. She was all he could think about. The softness of her curves pressing against his own. He was lost in a small smile, his mind hazy at the thought of being with her.

"I left you behind last time, Addy. I let you run away from me. I'm not letting you get away again. You belong with me." There was a longing for her that wouldn't fade away. He hated it, in a way. Nothing stopped her running again apart from his own speed, his own knowledge. He sighed softly, standing guard over her. He'd not let anything hurt her. He was waiting for her to wake up. He could watch her sleeping from his position outside her partially open window.

It was only when he heard a muffled, choked sob did he switch his attention from guarding her to the way she thrashed on the bed. She fought something unseen, screaming though the pillow stifled the sound. He realized if she woke up and saw him, he would appear crazy. He needed to court her again. Watching her move around and thrash, he felt sorrow and wanted to help. There was no way to know what terrors gripped her at night. Then she calmed down. Something washed over her and he knew she was dreaming of something pleasurable the way a smile danced across her lips, and then it was wiped away as she became terrified once more.

He couldn't watch anymore. He moved away from the window and decided to find her in a more normal setting in the morning. This way he could apologize for being so forward with her and try to make her understand his actions. It wouldn't be easy, but he could do it.

That night, he had a very hard time sleeping as he was gripped with desire one minute and panic over losing her again in the next. Finally, he woke and headed out to find her after a cold shower. It would be different this time. It had to be.

Addy sat sipping coffee in a small shop close to her house. He easily found her by following her scent and stood outside the coffee shop waiting to catch her eye. He tried to look like he was deciding between going across the road to a different diner and going into the coffee shop. When she caught his eye, he smiled shyly and walked into the coffee shop ready to try and gain her trust back.

He could tell she recognized him and averted her eyes when he walked in the door. So, he approached her and waited for her to speak.

"You freaked me out last night sir." She finally spoke after staring at him for a while wondering who he was or what he wanted with her. Her voice was just as soft and sweet as Adam remembered it to be. She was beautiful and perfect in every way. He wasn't stupid. He knew there was no way this could be the same girl he has fallen in love with and shown his true self to all those years ago – but, she looked just like her. She smelled like her too. Maybe, he was getting a second chance. A second chance at love. Besides the fact that she wouldn't remember who she was in a past life, she was still very much the same girl. It was a confusing thought for even him to wrap his head around, and he'd been around for centuries and knew the wonders of the world.

"Call me Adam, and I know. I'm really sorry about that." She was still guarded but her face had relaxed a bit so he considered that a good sign. "May I sit and explain myself."

She hesitated, but nodded and gestured across from her. Even though he had freaked her out and she couldn't decide whether he was a creep or someone who had made an honest mistake at not knowing who she was, there was something stirring inside of her that wanted to know more. Who was he? Why did he know her name? Was there another girl out there with the same name as her that looked just like her? So many burning questions she wanted him to answer. He knew all that was running through her mind because the past Addys had wanted to know the same thing. The three or four he'd managed to track down and successfully freak out. He was good at that.

"I'll give you five minutes." She was so feisty and independent just like he remembered her. She was Addy through and through, but he would get to that later.

"I thought you were someone else. My Addy was pretty like you, and she passed away. I just saw her in you and I lost myself for a minute. I'm really sorry, but you can't combine grief with alcohol. It was inappropriate what happened and I wish I could make it up to you."

She studied him and he wondered if she was buying it. "You knew my name. It's a coincidence my name is Addy, but it really scared me."

"Yes, I can see how that might. Let me buy you a coffee and make it up to you. Well, at least try to start."

She nodded and he ordered before deciding to engage her in conversation instead of leaving right away.

"How did she die?" She questioned with curious eyes.

"She became ill over time and then slipped away."

"I'm sorry, cancer sucks. I lost someone too. They died unexpectedly and it's hard when that happens. Sometimes, I have nightmares about it. You seem so young... I'm sorry you could lose your Addy at such a young age. There is never a good time for illness to take a life, but it is especially devastating to take someone at such a young age."

"I'm sorry that's very difficult." He smiled warmly and the waitress brought his coffee. The truth was, the last time as many times before when Addy had passed away, it was the sickness of old age, but that would be too difficult to explain to a mortal so he didn't.

"What do you do Adam," she changed the subject and he was pleased.

"I work in construction. I like to build things with my hands. It's been something I've always loved doing."

"I knew it had to be something like that. I could tell when you ran your hands over my skin you were a hard worker." She blushed realizing at what she'd said.

"Yes, I was inappropriate," he said remembering that night with fondness. Heat crept through him as he remembered how nice it had been to touch her. He pushed it down deep. They continued to talk about this and that. She was fascinating to him and he wanted to know everything about her. She was a research assistant and made her own hours. She loved her job but wanted more.

"You can do whatever you put your mind to. I know that for a fact." He said.

"I don't know Adam. You have some pretty crazy faith in someone you don't know at all."

"I would like to see you again, if that's okay Addy. I really enjoyed spending time with you." They had paid and were walking out the front door.

"Yes, I would like that Adam. Here's my number. Call me whenever." She smiled and he watched as she walked away from him back towards her apartment.

I can do this. I can date her until I have to reveal the truth to her again. At least, I will get to be with her again if only for a brief time.

It had been years since Adam felt even an ounce of happiness. In this moment, he was over the moon. He couldn't wait to spend more time with her. He knew she was the same Addy he had fallen in love with all of those years ago. He knew they were meant to be. If not, why had fate brought them together once again? Adam would do whatever he needed to do to make her love him again.

CHAPTER THREE

Addison went home to her apartment with a huge smile on her face. She was pleased the man who had made her feel so much passion on the dance floor wasn't the huge freak she thought he was. He was handsome and nice.

She could forgive a drunken mistake She had made them in the past, and who knew, maybe one day they would be telling a PG version of the story to their children. She still couldn't shake the feeling that she knew him somehow, someway.

When she was younger and asked her mother how she knew dad was it for her, she told her it would just be easy to be with them. Like you were supposed to be there, your best friends. Her mom had been right about a lot of things. Maybe, that's what she was feeling and she just thought it was familiar.

She really wished her mother was around now to give her grown up daughter advice. How she wished she'd soaked up so much wisdom and time from her mother when she was alive. The day was young and she had some errands to run, but she spent a large amount of time day dreaming on the couch. She wasn't going to over think this. She was just going to see where it went. If he turned out to be a weirdo chasing someone who passed away a long time ago, then she could simply get out.

After going to pick up her laundry, buying the week's groceries, and weeding the pathetic patch of grass outside her apartment, she felt a little tired. A nap wouldn't hurt her and she didn't have as many nightmares during the day. She fell into her bed setting an alarm for a couple of hours later knowing she'd be up long before then. Sleep came quickly and so did the dreams.

Addison stood in the bar with the sky open above it and music faintly playing in the distance. It sounded like harps, and not bar music. She wore a floor length dress with her hair piled tall on her head. She could feel the weight of it as she went to turn and take in her surroundings. He moved up behind her before she noticed his presence and wrapped a hand around her waist swaying with her to the music. The bar was empty and larger than she remembered. He twirled her and suddenly they were in a castle. It was massive with pillars everywhere and he pulled her to him. The ceiling was really tall, and paintings covered each wall.

"Addy my love, my sweet lass. I must show you something and I don't want you to become scared or run away from me."

"Stop being silly Adam. I could never run from you."

The sadness in his eyes gave her pause. She thought the whole situation felt very familiar. He pulled his hands from hers and backed up into the middle of the room. It was quick. One minute her Adam stood in front of her, and the next, a large dragon replaced him. Terror seized her chest, it couldn't be.

She ran and cried and ran as far as she could. When she reached the edge of the forest she'd run through, she saw the dragon again. The dream shifted and she was in an arena watching him. He was fighting another bright red dragon and she felt fear for him.

"Father, this is ridiculous," she yelled at an older man wearing a long cape and a huge gold crown.

"This is how they have chosen to fight for your hand Adeline. This is how it should be."

The two dragons clashed and fought in front of her while she watched in fear. Her lover Sam was not as strong as that brute Adam and he would surely perish.

The dream shifted again and she was running through a forest, but wore a different dress than the first dream and her hair was long and braided over one shoulder.

"Darling, let me explain." Adam chased her through the woods and she just wanted to get away from him. The dream shifted again and she stood in the middle of a field watching herself in the three scenes surrounding her and playing over and over. How many times had this happened? She awoke feeling confused and not sure what any of it meant.

Maybe she was dreaming of Adam as a dragon because he was going to protect her. A dragon was a type of protector. She was pleased that the nightmares were replaced with these nightmares. They were scary but not as much as the car accidents were.

Her phone dinged and she rolled over to look at it surprised to see she had slept almost the entire two hours. She never did that, and the dreams had seemed so fast.

I can't wait to see you again. I figured a text was less presumptuous than calling immediately.

She wouldn't have minded if he called immediately, but it was cute that he thought about how she might view it if he did. It was surprising to her that she found it difficult to find the words to respond. Finally, she sent back something well thought out and prolific.

Me neither.

Well, at least it was something. She smiled to herself and clutched the phone to her chest waiting for his reply. Maybe that's why he seemed so familiar to her, because she'd dreamed of him somehow. That didn't make sense though. How would she know to dream about him if she'd never actually seen him?

His response was quick. How about tomorrow I take you to a play and then we go to dinner?

She didn't even know there were plays in the area, at least she'd never been to one. Her phone beeped again.

Full disclosure it's my godson's play so it might not be the type you are used to going to.

Sounds perfect. Her heart melted a little as she thought of Adam playing with little kids.

She finally dove into her book in between answering emails from her boss and his client. It was nice that she could work from home and enjoy a little bit of peace. When the time to quit finally came, she was almost through the book and made herself a sandwich.

Going to sleep that night, she thought the nightmares might be replaced with the same dragon and old timey dreams from early, but as soon as her eyes closed, the screeching of metal and the sounds of breaking bones filled her head. She woke up in the morning shaking and sweating.

"So much for having kind of good dreams more than once," she said. At least she had the play to look forward to. She would enjoy spending time with Adam and seeing what he was like when he wasn't apologizing for being a horny insane male. She decided it wasn't too early to get her outfit for the evening in order and went to play in her closet.

CHAPTER FOUR

He picked her up and looked amazing as he had before. He wore a nicer polo shirt and khakis which made her delighted at the simple casual blue dress she'd chosen.

"You look gorgeous lass, as always."

She felt heat creep up into her cheeks and looked down. "You look great as well."

He held his arm out for her to take and she did. They walked to his car a simple little sports car in black and he held the door open for her.

"I saw you as a truck kind of man," she said as he got in with her.

"Really? I've never owned one. Like the simple things I guess." They pulled out and went to the Elementary school for the play he'd been talking about. It's Jordan's big play debut. He keeps calling it that. He plays a tree so I'm fairly certain he doesn't speak. He's really excited about it."

"Then I'm sure he'll be wonderful."

Adam's friend Sam waited for them in the second row.

"This is Addison Moore. Addison, this is Samuel Crowe, one of my oldest and dearest friends."

"Pleasure Addison." Sam looked familiar. She couldn't place him and spent a lot of time glancing over at him. Adam noticed, but he didn't say anything. Finally, when it hit her, it hit her hard. He was in her dream. How the hell was he also in her dream?

It was starting to make her feel like she was losing her mind but then the children on stage started to sing and Adam took her hand. She was lulled into a secure place and tried to put it out of her head.

They stood and applauded loudly so the children knew they appreciated their performance.

"Your son is too adorable," she gushed to Sam trying not to look him in the eyes since all she thought of was the dream.

"Thank you so much for coming," the little boy ran up to his Dad in tree form and jumped into his arms.

"Hey Uncle Adam, thanks for coming to my big debut." He swept his hand wide so he included the whole theatre and jumped into Adam's arms.

"Jordan here is a whole eight years old this month Addy."

"I like your name," the little boy leaned into Adam's chest shyly and she couldn't help but smile. Where was that little boy who had commanded the whole gymnasium to watch him as a tree? She didn't say anything about that though.

"I like your name too."

"Let's go eat." Adam kissed Jordan on the top of his branches and passed him back to Sam. He leaned in and whispered something to Adam, but she couldn't hear what it was. He took her back to the car, opening the door for her, and drove to a little restaurant overlooking a pond.

"You can feed the ducks," he told her as they got out and went into the little restaurant. He had made reservations and the quaint little restaurant was very private. The booths were isolated with candles burning in the middle of the tables and on the walls.

"I'm underdressed for this," she said as she slid into the booth.

"There's no dress code here Addy," he smiled and pointed to something on the menu for the waiter to bring them. Soon, their table had wine and appetizers. They fell into easy conversation like they always did and Addy felt completely at ease. She was happy she had given him another chance and not let first impression run her life.

After they ate, he took her out back to look over the pond. He kissed her cheek and went to put a quarter into the feeding machines. She saw two ducks at first, but as soon as she started to spread the feed in the water, they all came running.

"Look at them all," she said cheerfully as they clamoured over each other to get to the food. It was a truly great date, and she couldn't get over how romantic Adam was. He'd thought the date out completely.

"You bait me with your cute as hell godson and then bring me to feed ducks. You knew what you were doing didn't you?" She asked laughing.

"Imagine if you hated children and ducks. I took a chance." He wrapped his arms around her waist as she continued spreading the food over the water. There were babies mixed in with the adult ducks and her heart simply melted when she saw them.

It was a lot of fun watching them eat, and she barely noticed a few rain drops were falling. The rain came suddenly down in sheets and the ducks quacked as they flew around and moved out into the water to catch the fish jumping up to get the rain drops.

They ran back to the car completely soaking wet and laughed. Once they were inside the car, he reached over and took her face in his hands. He pressed his lips to hers and wrapped her up tightly in his arms. Not caring about the water dripping off of them, she returned the kiss.

She felt taken completely over by desire the second his tongue entered her mouth. He explored and kissed her deeply while his fingers dug into her hips. He pulled her closer and she returned his kiss hungry for it, wrapping her arms around him, and bringing him as close to her as she could.

The warmth of his body surrounded her like an invisible blanket. It was searing into her body. His essence moved with the heat and poured through her. She felt something spark in her brain and pulled away from him. It was another feeling of familiarity, and what she'd felt in her dreams, but she was wide awake now.

Her vision blurred around the edges and she saw him scaly clothed in purple iridescent scales across the forest. She shook her head and thought she saw a change in him but then she was back to looking at him directly in front of her. It was him but he was dressed as he was from her dream and looking down at herself so was she. Then they changed again and she gasped.

***

She was looking at him but she wasn't there. It was as if she staring far off into the distance.

"Addy darling, what's wrong," He shook her gently.

"I just had a déjà vu. I'm sure it's nothing." She shook her head back and forth as if to clear the thought and smiled at him.

"So, you're saying my kisses remind you of another man," he teased.

"Not at all," she slapped his chest playfully. "I just felt like I've been here in this place before. Does that ever happen to you?"

"More than I like," he said sadly.

"The play was lovely, and your godson played that tree with the passion of a much older actor." She smiled sweetly.

"He's a card, but he's a great kid. I love how he improvised and swayed. His Dad told me that wasn't in the script."

She giggled. "I need to get home. I have to be in an actual face to face meeting tomorrow. Something tells me I'll sleep well tonight."

He wasn't sure what she meant by that but nodded and held out his arm to escort her back to the car. He'd held onto his tongue and not said anything that could be construed as creepy. His friend had eyed him a bit when he introduced Addy and he was sure Sam knew exactly who she was. At one point, many years ago, they had been enemies. One lifetime Sam was Adeline's lover and he'd killed him in a battle for her hand. She'd never forgiven him and that was how he'd lost her in that lifetime. Of course, Sam wasn't dead. You can't kill a dragon that easily, but he was ready to hide from the thought of getting married. That was a terrible time for him, but when Adeline had grown older and Adam realized that this was not the life he would spend with her, Sam and him had become friends and never fought over her again.

He had winked at him knowing Adam would have to tell her, and he whispered good luck to him when they parted ways.

Over dinner, Addy had gushed over Sam and thought he looked familiar. It was interesting how see remembered glimmers. That night, he kissed her and left her knowing he would probably be back later, unable to sleep and watching her toss and turn with her nightmares. He had to have patience and let her get to know him better this time, perhaps even fall in love with him again before he sprang it on her.

The next couple of weeks, he courted her and it was a nice time. He didn't feel like he was smothering her and he kept all his thoughts about their past lives to himself. He was falling deep and hoped she was as well.

CHAPTER FIVE

Late one night, Addison couldn't stop the scream from passing her lips when she woke up. Her breathing was erratic and sweat had rolled down her temples. She felt helpless as she brought her knees to her chest and tried to stop the sobbing from wracking her small frame. All she could do was replay the nightmare in her mind. She was unsure what to do with herself. She forced herself out of her bed. She felt drawn to look out her window. He was there. She didn't know why or how, but he was there.

When she saw him standing there, she felt as though her pain was soothed and melted away. She had recognized him from their previous meeting. Addison nudged her white-framed window open slightly and peered out. Her red hair sliding from her shoulders.

"Hello again Adam." She smiled and leaned her cheek in her hand. In that moment, Addy's heart felt as though it would both stop and never stop racing. She didn't even think to question why he was outside her window so late at night.

He shifted his weight as he spoke, "Addy my lass, do you want to stroll with me?" Adam knew that his Addy was always comforted while amongst the trees.

She tried to reason with herself. Addison knew she should rest but something within her longed to be out in nature. "Hmm..." She giggled and allowed the noise to travel towards him infecting him with joy. "I'll be down in a bit!"

The bathroom mirror projected Addison's reflection as she cleaned her face quickly. She tried to suppress a smile. There was something about Adam that made her feel so young and almost naïve. She rushed down and greeted him once more. Since she was more familiar with him, she wasn't frightened of him at all.

Together they walked towards the nature path. Adam nudged her on the path slightly. He did so teasingly because he longed to touch her. Any part of her.

She suddenly broke the silence as she told him, "I have to say, I don't normally go for walks with men in the middle of the night. I think you should consider yourself lucky." She wouldn't have with any other man, she thought. He felt familiar, safe, and in some way, as though she was meant to be near him.

He watched her speak, his eyes locked on her lips. He opened his mouth to reply to her but he heard something rustling. She could tell by the way he moved towards the trees and cocked his head to listen. "Addy, lass, don't move…" He pushed his body towards her own to protect her.

"What? I don't hear-" Adam quickly pressed his hand to her mouth.

In front of them on the trail was a giant bear. The bear looked almost demonic in expression as it faced the pair. It unleashed a giant growl that made Addison clench Adam's shirt tightly. Her breathing became tense with fear.

Addison cried out and tried to grasp at him. Her fear turned into panic and soon turned into screams. The bear was so menacing and he was coming right for them. Finally, the feeling of fear overtook her and she fainted.

Addison awoke with the cold earth underneath her and the sun blocked from her view. Where was she? The better question was where the bear, that had just been there moments ago, was. Although her mind raced with these thoughts she did not feel panicked. Addison saw the glimmer of what appeared to be scales above her. She felt the pressure atop of her, yet it did not hurt. Trying to get her bearings, she couldn't figure out for the life of her what was going on.

***

Adam had tried to suppress his inner anger, his other side begging to come out. It needed to come out to protect his Addy. He had successfully scared the bear away, but now, he'd shown his true self to his beloved. He hoped no one else had seen him when he changed and knew he would have to face her and see if she would once again run away from him.

His fury had taken over him. He could not allow for his Addy to be hurt. The beast within him had transformed him and enslaved his body once again. He had managed to transform himself without crushing his beloved. He felt his claw atop of her. His eyes closed as he felt Addison touch his talons. She felt the talons, the smooth yet sharp edge that did not pierce her. This calmed him.

He was able to transform back into his human body, unsure of how much she actually saw. Within moments, his body was on top of hers.

She tried to speak, to ask what had happened. "I just, I don't-" she stammered.

"Hush my lass" Adam whispered to her. He gazed into her ever green eyes and put his hand in her hair. He ran his fingers through the soft tresses. Addison's gaze lowered as she calmed beneath him and allowed him to press his lips on to hers.

Although his eyes were shut, they stung with tears he held back. He brushed his lips onto hers and whispered to her "Addy... my dear." He kissed her again before he continued. "I thought I'd lost you forever."

Adam then pressed his lips lightly on to hers. His mouth moved towards her neck as he kissed her there as one of his hands entangled within hers. Addison's hips turned and pushed into him as she moved closer. The desire that he felt was almost uncontrollable, but he wanted to enjoy it. Adam fed off her energy that was exuding towards him. His other hand moved towards her shoulder. He quickly slipped off her straps to expose her collar bone and shoulders to his teeth. Adam's lips never left her skin as he gently bit her now exposed shoulder. Addison moaned as she moved her head to expose more of her skin to him. He had waited for so long, and now, she would be his once more.

She was scared and unbelieving of what she saw, but her desire had taken over and he could feel it rush through him as she allowed him to touch her. He would tell her everything after he loved her.

CHAPTER SIX

Addison felt beyond confused by his words. What could he mean by that? He'd thought he lost her that night at the bar, in his dreams, what? Her mind filled with questions yet her body accepted what he was doing to her. Her cold lips were instantly warmed by his. His skin felt so hot compared to hers. Addison placed her hands around his neck as she kissed him deeply.

She felt the fire in her burn as she longed for his body. Adam could feel her desire as her skin grew hot with each passionate kiss they shared. She longed for him to touch her more. She needed Adam to calm the beast within her that grew with each passing moment. Her body burned with desire towards him and she needed him to touch her.

His mouth moved towards her neck as he kissed her there as one of his hands entangled within one of her own. Addison's hips seemed to move on their own as they pushed themselves closer to his. This burning desire within her for Adam started to almost hurt with pressure between her legs.

Her once racing mind had seemed to be quickly calmed with each passing moment with Adam. Nothing mattered at this moment except that she needed more of him. Addison grabbed Adam's hand and placed it on her breast and gasped as the peak hardened to his touch. He soon ran his fingertips beneath her shirt. He lingered on her breast, tweaking the nipple to torment her as he moved his lips back to her own. Addison let out a moan as she grabbed at his waist.

Adam pulled away from their kiss and continued to slide her shirt off of her. He allowed it to pool at her waist, her breast almost exposed except for her blush coloured bra. Adam's hips pressed themselves into his Addy's. She let out a small moan as she felt his hard member. Her hands slowly traced their way down his torso and thumbed the fabric that bulged.

Addison's body begged for more. She struggled for words as her breath was quick and shallow. No one had made her feel this good before. She had become quickly addicted to the feeling he was providing her. She craved more of Adam and he cupped her at the apex of her thighs sending sensations throughout her. She buckled under him and let out a long moan.

"Adam!" she gasped. "I need you." Addison moaned as he went slower to tease her. Adam pushed down his briefs and stroked himself allowing Addison to see him fully. She eyed him hungrily as she moved her hips and squirmed waiting for him. Adam climbed on top of her and pushed her panties to the side. Allowing the tip to slowly rub against her. "And, I need you." He whispered into her ear as he pushed the tip into her.

Addison grasped at his shoulders and moaned deeply when he filled her with himself. His fit was perfect for her. His member filled her perfectly. She could feel him pulsing as he waited for her to adjust to him. Soon, he began to thrust into her slowly. Each one felt better than the last. She bit her lip to suppress a small squeal of delight. Adam grabbed her legs and placed them on his shoulders. This position allowed him to watch her face fill with pleasure as he pushed himself deeper into her.

Addison moved a hand to her mouth biting on her finger. She didn't want to be too loud nor did she want to let screams escape her lips. Addison wanted to keep each pleasure noise deep within her so she could relish in the moment.

They moved in unison. Allowing the warmth of their bodies to spread to the other. Adam then moved to press his torso onto hers as he buried his head in her neck and hair. Addison's fingers found their way into his shoulder blades. Her finger tips digging into his skin as she was unable to stop herself. She moaned as Adam sped up his thrusts and they became heavier. He could feel her coming close to the brink of no return and he was determined to ensure she got there.

Addison's breath became shallow and erratic. Her stomach clenching and her body tense. "I'm... I'm..." she stammered as she continuously moaned. Her body riding each wave of pleasure that radiated throughout her.

Once her breathing had returned to a somewhat normal pace, she propped herself up and looked over at him.

"What are you Adam, tell me? I know what I saw, but I don't believe it," she whispered. "Dragons don't exist."

He pulled her into his arms and petted her hair. "Oh but my darling lass, they do indeed exist. Let me tell you a story."

He held her close and cleared his throat before telling her about his many lives. "Addy, I found you a long time ago. I loved you with all of my heart, but fate intervened and we were not able to be together." He sighed and his voice got a little shaky and sad before he continued. He didn't really like thinking about this story, let alone reliving it. But, she needed to know about everything. He explained she was always running from him no matter what life they were in, and in some, even if she accepted the dragon in him, it was another she pined for.

All of the nightmares and dreams she had been having started to make sense. Even though it was unbelievable to her and the dreams didn't make sense when she was having them. They made sense now. She was dreaming about all of her past lives. She had read about reincarnation before. She had always thought about how cool of a theory it was to think about, but she never dreamed it could really happen. Yet, here she was, an actual reincarnation. It was a lot to take in, but she knew she wanted to be with him. It wasn't that scary knowing he was there to help her make sense of it all.

"I'm not running this time. I don't know why, but I can feel that you're telling the truth and know that you are a good man. I don't have anyone else in my life anymore."

CHAPTER SEVEN

As amazing as those words felt to hear, he had a hard time believing there was any truth to them. He remembered where she was and what she was doing the night he found her. She was surrounded by friends. She was not going to leave the people in her life to be with him.

"That can't be true. You have friends you were with the night I met you." He finally spoke up after being so deep in thought. He didn't want her to give up her life to be with him. Sure, he wanted to be with her. He wanted nothing more than that. But, she had a life – and he wasn't part of it. At least, he finally got to tell her the truth and she didn't run away from him this time. He could live with that. It was a much happier ending than the one he had had all those years ago.

"There weren't any friends with me. I was just dancing with people. My brother, sister, and parents were killed in a car accident and I was the only one who survived." He could hear the sadness in her voice as she explained why she didn't have anyone in her life worth sticking around for.

"I'm sorry. Those are the nightmares you are having?" He asked in a sweet and sincere voice. Now that he stopped and thought about it, he hadn't really seen her with anyone since the night that he first found her. Was she really all alone in the world? Maybe she was just waiting for him to find her again? Maybe this was fate?

"Yes, but since you started coming around, I've had other dreams, and I think they were of my past lives running from you."

He smiled at her and kissed the top of her head. "I want to be with you and you won't have to worry about waking from those dreams by yourself anymore."

"I want to be with you too."

"Let's create our own family, and you won't be alone anymore." He said as he ran his hands over her arms. She turned to him and smiled.

"Alright," she wiggled her brows. "We can start right now." She pulled him to her and kissed him deeply soaking in the feeling and happy to have finally found her other half.

"I have a silly question." She whispered breaking the deep kiss they were sharing. He smiled and caressed her cheek. "Ask me anything."

"What happens when we have children, I mean if we have children of course?" She felt silly and stupid for asking the question, but she was curious as to how dragons were born in the first place. If she had children with him, would they be dragons or would they be humans? She wasn't asking because she didn't want to have dragon babies with him, she was asking because she was curious.

Adam couldn't help but laugh at the question. It was refreshing to have this Addy back. This curious Addy who burned to know everything about everything. "It's not a silly question." He whispered. "If we have children together, then they could be like you and simply live their lives as humans, or they could be like me and share the dragon gene. I'd be completely happy either way.

She flashed another smile happy that he was so forthcoming with answering her questions and he loved that she was so curious about it. It was so much better than having her be terrified of what would happen. "I will answer all of your questions about me, my dear. As long as you promise never to run away from me. I will tell you everything that you want to know."

She grabbed his face and kissed him deeply one more time before turning her face to his ear. "Show me" She whispered. "I want you to show me your dragon form. I'm not going to run away from you – not ever."

He blushed a bit before standing up and peeling off his clothing. He would be lying if he didn't admit to feeling nerves in the pit of his stomach. He remembered this scenario replaying in his head the first time he showed Addy his true form. She wanted nothing to do with him. She thought he was a monster.

He took a deep breath and exploded before her. Suddenly, a huge dragon was standing near her. His large talons creasing the ground as he exhaled a few puffs of steam. She stood up and walked over to him. She wasn't afraid because she knew he wouldn't hurt her. She walked right over to him and ran her hand across his scaly body. Petting him as if he was her pet.

He quickly turned back into his human form standing before her stark naked. He wasted no time scooping her up and embracing her. "I love you Addy. I want to spend the rest of my life with you." He whispered before kissing her deeply. This. This was a much better ending to his story of telling her the truth.

EPILOGUE

About a year later...

"I'm sleepy love."

"I know sweetheart, sleep for a while. I'll stay up and feel the kicks." He pressed his hands to her stomach and felt his son's powerful kicks.

"He's going to be a strong dragon, like his father," she smiled at him, and he shook his head.

"We don't know that's true. It could just as easily be that he has no dragon in him."

"I can feel it," Addy said, "I know it will be true. What will happen when I grow old and die?"

"Why would you think about such things now?" He asked and pushed hair away from her face to plant a kiss on her forehead.

"It's been on my mind. If our son is dragon, he will outlive me as well. I have to think about these things Adam. If I didn't, I wouldn't be human." Her eyes suddenly grew big. "Will he come out a dragon? How will I go to a hospital and have a dragon, oh my God, how big will he be?"

"No, dear." Adam rubbed her back trying to calm her. "Whether he's a dragon or not he will come into the world a fully human-looking, normal-sized baby. You don't have to worry and we can go through with our regular hospital plan."

"Oh, okay. That's a relief, can you imagine?" she shivered and thought about the fact that a dragon could burst from her and tried not to think about it too much.

Addison had remembered their past lives together as she became more connected to her dragon. He was a window into the past, and each time they were together, she remembered more realizing they were truly supposed to be together. She apologized profusely for running from him all those years ago and promised she would do her best to never do it again.

"I'll find you in your next life, just as I found you in this one. Each time your scent is the same even if you look different, and if you run, I will find you in the next one."

"I can't think about it."

"Then don't sweetheart. Let's just be in the moment and enjoy it okay. The child will be here soon and we won't have the time to muse over life. We'll barely be able to hold our heads up."

"I can't wait Adam," she grinned and kissed him sweetly.

"I can't either sweetheart, now go to sleep." Holding her husband with one hand and her belly with the other, Addy fell into a restful sleep, the nightmares replaced with blissful dreams of the past and future.

The End

ABOUT THE AUTHOR

Milena Fenmore is a small business owner who lives in the world of the paranormal. Deeply interested in all things supernatural and a hopeless romantic, she has found her true passion as an indie author of paranormal romance. Knowing what a true romance reader wants, Milena is intent on helping her readers experience love and passion through her writing, creating a mystical world they can revel in.

Printed in Great Britain
by Amazon